THE WANDERERS 3.0
THE ICE ON THE TOWER

SARTHAK RATHI

ISBN 979-8-88869-640-8

Contents

Prologue *5*

Acknowledgements *11*

Chapter 1   The Rescue 13

Chapter 2   Gas Really be Exploding.......................... 20

Chapter 3   The Edge.................................... 33

Chapter 4   Amnesia.................................... 49

Chapter 5   Recalling
An Year Later 56

Chapter 6   Space 64

Chapter 7   Abduction.................................... 80

Chapter 8   Magic DNA 89

Chapter 9   Blizzards. And Birds…?.......................... 104

Chapter 10   Abduction. Again 117

Chapter 11   Ooh Frosty.................................... 137

Chapter 12   The Ice on the Tower 147

Epilogue *163*

Prologue

*2019, C-11 (Marsars), just before the Tiaras' house
blew up in Denmark*

The General had been alive for seven thousand years, something not even the Great Warlocks were able to accomplish. He owed this to stolen Technomagic from across the Milky Way and some Dark Magic. He wasn't a bad person, even though Dark Magic was outlawed. By the General himself, no less. He wanted to stop Soundleek Hanginton from blowing up Earth's moon. Because it was their next potential residence.

They had been living on Marsars for five thousand years, after they were chased away from their own planet by the Xinains, after an ancient thousand-year war. The General had witnessed the war in its entirety. He had seen cities and countries wiped out. It had been hell. Two species inhabited Xin, the planet the Marsians had lived on before: The Marsians and the Xinains. The Marsians had been losing that war, and finally had been kicked off the planet. The people who hadn't fought in the war suffered the most.

They had found a home here, a planet about 5 billion years old, and miraculously it still had a supercontinent. It was starting to break down, but the Marsians would be long gone by then, because the planet was about to blow up.

The scientists had made a weird discovery. They couldn't penetrate the planet to its core. Since the Marsians had the proper tech to go to planets' cores, this was weird. What they had found was bizarre and defied all laws of physics. The core was held together by natural magnets, which made the gravity of this planet insanely difficult to deal with, but the Marsians had adapted. Nobody except the General remembered how difficult it was to establish the first few cities. So many structures had fallen. So much testing.

The planet would blow up because of the constantly filling up *Mizrom* gas. It was a highly flammable gas, and nickel and cobalt were highly reactive when exposed to it. The gas had been accumulating around the core for some time. The General knew they would have to move to another place in the next five to ten weeks. Currently, he was sitting in his office, talking with Jammari, his head scientist, also the Whizari's head scientist.

He had been with the Marsians for the last ten years, and the General had to give it to him for not getting caught all that time. But that time was coming close, since Jammari was planning to completely abandon the Whizari. He had been equipped with a chip of Marsian tech not available to anybody else. The chip was pure magic. When it was broken, it could take you to the place it had been assigned to. In this case, Marsars. Jammari had never had to use it before, but the General had a feeling it would come in handy soon.

The General gestured to Jammari. "How long do you give this planet?"

"Eh, about seven to eight weeks?"

They were talking about a planet exploding like it was a bet. The threat was imminent, and the damage was minimal. They could do nothing but joke about it. The Marsians had long perfected Nanotech and could pretty much pack all of it in literal suitcases without damaging its contents. And carry it with them like clothes on a vacation.

Jammari said, "Where are you going, anyways?" Jammari interrupted his train of thought and picked a glass of water from the table.

"To the moon," The General said. He thought Jammari knew, but forgot how long it had been since he had seen his informant.

Jammari spat some water out. "We can't go there."

"The Strike on the Satellite won't be happening, Jammari," The General said. "I am making sure that she will be stopped."

Jammari nodded and got up from his seat. "Well, I better be on my way."

"Where?" The General said.

"Well, back to H'vannat. The attack's still tomorrow, right?"

The General nodded. "Tomorrow."

"Are the troops ready?"

The General nodded.

"I am still doubtful the Strike on the Satellite will be delayed because of this attack."

"That is not my only motive, Jammari." Jammari looked at the General expectantly but got no answer. He sighed and left the office, and the door closed after him. The General wanted to get some grudges out of the way.

* * *

Due to the assistance of the Nameri, the attack wasn't particularly difficult. The fact that it had to be a Marsian attack limited the firepower they could use. There was even a point where the Marsians were almost at the verge of losing. But the attack had gone well, and the General was positive the Strike on the Satellite had been delayed, because the Whizari were preparing for their attack on the Marsians. And the exploding planet had been preponed, happening in the next two weeks. It was bad, but technology couldn't really stop planets from exploding in on itself.

Nearly a billion people would be leaving in a flurry, in a day. That was expensive and difficult, but the Marsians had been prepared for it for a long time. If they had to leave in five minutes, it would happen.

The General currently was walking alone in a park. The general had been to Earth, disguised, and had found out that humans and the Marsians had pretty similar ways of thinking. They weren't aware of the consequences they could be facing, but the General was sure that they could convince humans of their harmfulness.

Jammari suddenly appeared next to the General, with a car. It hovered over the grass. This wasn't allowed, but since the park was really empty, the General shrugged it off.

"So, why are you out here alone?" Jammari said. "Also, my stomach's almost okay, thanks for asking."

Jammari had been stabbed, and if not for the chip, he would have surely been dead. Soundleek Hanginton had probably guessed he was alive, but he was safe for now. The Strike on the Satellite was still happening, and the General had just sparked a war with the Whizari. They could get something out of that war, but Soundleek Hanginton was getting more.

The General had a feeling that Soundleek Hanginton knew about the magic of the Marsians. How she knew, he had no clue, and couldn't begin to fathom what the consequences would be if she managed to do what he thought she was going to do.

But that was supposed to be impossible, wasn't it?

The General turned to say something to Jammari, but heard a distinct *BOOM!*

"It's happening right now," The General whispered.

The General and Jammari just stood there for a second, trying to hear any more explosions, but for now, this seemed to be it. They looked at each other again, with dread.

They ran.

Five minutes later, ships were leaving in a hurry, leaving their beloved planet behind. The General's eyes glistened, and it was the first time in millennia that he had cried. Jammari stood beside him, solemnly watching the planet explode.

They were now a distance from the planet that the planet appeared to be the size of a tennis ball. A huge explosion rocked the ship.

Marsars was no more.

Acknowledgements

So many people helped me in the process. I believe Notion Press and its publishing team for getting this book out. Incredibly grateful for you guys.

My wonderful mom, who was the primary reason this book came out, albeit kinda late. Thank you for letting me play shooting games.

My awesome dad, who was there for us all throughout the terrible pandemic. Thank you for giving me this edgy humour.

My brother, who I miss so much, giving me invaluable advice, while managing a busy schedule 13500 kilometres away.

My family, who have always been there for me. Always gonna love y'all.

My school, without which I never would have gotten where I am.

My friends. Even though none of you are gonna read this, I love you guys.

And last but not the least, my readers, the people who have picked up the third book. Thank you so much.

CHAPTER 1

The Rescue

PARI

Fragments of wall flew around us. We ducked. I waited for another explosion, but it never came.

"It's gone." I heard a growl and recognized it as Hanginton's voice. Her voice sounded like she was on the verge of crying. She started shouting at the people who worked for her (of course she wasn't going to blame herself for being arrogant enough to let literal children get past her) before chaos ensued.

The glass above us broke.

We had one moment to look at the rushing water before it would come down to kill us. That never happened.

Three conical ships landed in the middle of the debris of the cannons. Doors silently lowered, and out of it emerged people clad in black armor. They shot the people behind Hanginton, and suddenly a wall emerged, blocking us off from Hanginton.

I was thankful the Marsians had decided to spare the lives of Hanginton's men. I had a feeling the people with Hanginton wouldn't have been alive if it had been an action movie, which made me wonder why action movies were more realistic than this.

The gaping hole above us was still there. A force field, probably. But the speed with which it was deployed, without letting even a droplet of water on us, was impressive.

As that crossed my mind, a drop of water fell on my cheek.

I shrugged and went back to my friends.

Glenda was smiling, and someone came from the ships and they shook hands. I didn't know who it was, but from the way the people were looking at him, he was someone important. He looked like us. Us as in the people of Earth. He was just a taller than any average human. All of the Marsians that were with him were tall. All of them were at least more than 7 feet, with large body builds.

Or I was just looking at all the tall people of that planet.

Probably not.

I went to stand with Sarthak. Anu and Yash were beside us too. Gertrude looked shook for some reason.

We were quickly ushered into the ships, without being informed about what the hell was going on. Adrenaline still ran inside me. The rush of destroying the machine, and the moon almost being destroyed. There was still the matter of how Hanginton figured out a way of destroying the moon that didn't involve global annihilation. Probably magic, like each and everything unnatural we had come across. This seemed like lazy writing on the part of whoever had written us into this hell.

The ship was in no way attractive, just a big hunk o' metal, practical in every way. It was filled to the brim with people, and as soon as the door closed behind us, it shot out of the hole it had made like a rocket. There was a whirring noise and through the potholes on the sides of the ship, I saw us descending out of water, only for a split second, we were out in a flash, leaving the blue dot of the lake behind.

Before I knew it, we were in the clouds, and the ship stopped ascending. I went to stand near my friends.

I looked at Anu and as usual, her hair was perfect. *How in the hell* – I decided to calm down. I was really agitated for some reason, I gave myself consolation by looking at Sarthak, who's hair resembled a bowl of noodles.

"Well, that was crazy," Yash said.

"Is that so, Captain obvious?" I said sarcastically in a deadpan voice. He gave me an irritated look.

Yash was pissed. "Who pissed in your breakfast?"

I smiled right back at him.

Sarthak clapped Yash on the shoulder for the hell of it. Yash winced and cursed at Sarthak really loudly. People gave him weird looks.

"So, what're we gonna do now?" I said to Gertrude, who was passing by.

"What exactly do you expect for an answer?" she was cut off by a distant boom, and the whole ship shook. Through the potholes, I saw a cloud of smoke, and realized that there was a force field around the ship keeping it protected. We all would have probably been dead if not for that thing. I took a deep breath.

"Not again," Sarthak groaned.

It was most definitely Hanginton. I wanted to headbutt her right in her nose. I felt better with that thought in my mind. The ship shook again, and I held on to the chair beside. Where the hell did that come from? The chair, I mean, not the attack. I was pretty sure the attack was from Hanginton.

"The *Sakuris!*" someone yelled. Either this was a code word for Hanginton, or something else I did not know about was attacking us.

"The *what*?" Anu said next to me. Why she thought the three of us or Clove would know, I didn't understand. I also didn't understand why I was having random thoughts. When someone was panicking, it tended to happen. I decided to change my train of thought or I was gonna go crazy.

"Everyone who is not going to fight, follow me!" a Marsian said. We followed her into a round-shaped room. There were chairs, and the room was itself bigger than the whole ship should have been. I remembered from the dreams that the Marsians had – well, awesome – advancements in nano-tech, but experiencing it was different. I felt like I was being deflated, and I didn't know what being deflated felt like, so I decided not to ponder over it.

I got into a seat and the seatbelts automatically secured themselves. Sarthak was on my right and Anu on my left, Yash to her left. Clove and her parents were sitting together, and so were Glenda and Gertrude. It felt like we were in an auditorium, waiting for someone to show up and talk about things. Completely unrelated to all this, I was feeling sick.

The whole ship shook again as something from below it hit and there was another *BOOM!* I held on the armrest so hard I was afraid it might come off, but then again, this wasn't a movie theatre and this wasn't, well, a frickin movie. I shook my head to get the sluggish thoughts out.

But we suddenly took off, the ship growled, and boom we were rushing towards space. We were getting out of there. That meant the people who were in the pods, fighting to defend us, were probably handled from this ship. They must have been like the Whizari pods. I wondered if we were gonna go to Marsars. The thought of visiting a new planet annoyed.

It was also dangerous, but I decided to keep that in the back of my mind. For now, I decided to try not to puke. I gripped Sarthak's hand. We were always close in a way most siblings aren't. Like, hugging and stuff. Normal siblings don't do that. Normal siblings slap you when you try to hug them.

We were now floating in space, and I could see the earth from the ship.

"It's beautiful," Glenda whispered.

I agreed with her. It was also scary, the vastness of space. When did I start having thoughts like these? This adventure really did something to all of us, and it's only been a few days. How did that happen?

Sarthak, sitting beside me, said, "Well *this* was unexpected."

I looked at him with a disgusted expression. "You sayin' this *now*?"

He grinned, glad to have infuriated me. He also texted me for some reason, just a single **:D**. I wanted to punch him for that, and I did.

"Ow!" was his response.

The ship suddenly started humming and we were pushed back into our seats as it suddenly rocketed through space. All I saw was black and blue in the windows, and then... nothing. The windows closed and for a moment I thought about the vastness of space, how it will never end. I decided to stop thinking about that before I went insane.

Sarthak and I were still holding hands, and he had the same look of fascination I was pretty sure I had. I had never thought that I would get to be here, in space, going to another fricking planet.

Before I knew it, I fell asleep, the constant humming of the ship in the background.

When I woke up, the ship wasn't moving anymore, we were floating in space, and we were next to a planet. Well, not a planet, but several pieces of it. It looked like it had exploded, but from what? And this sure wasn't Star Wars since I had seen no Light Sabers, but I didn't know what to expect anymore. I wondered why we had come to this wasteland of a planet, and what we would do here.

"What the heck?" Sarthak and Yash said at the same time, but I supressed by rage at the word, because I wanted to say the same exact thing. The planet still had some traces of green, but I was pretty sure that those were some, well, leftovers. I didn't have any words for what I was seeing.

"What happened?" Gertrude said.

"The planet exploded," Glenda said. She received disgusted looks. "Well, it's a long story." She told us about the *Mizrom* stuff, and also didn't know how that was possible. The fact that a planet could explode because of gas made no sense to me, but a lot of things didn't and well, they happened.

Someone came in and announced that we should get out of the room. Our seatbelts disappeared and we got up. For some reason, my legs felt like jelly. I wondered how long we had been in this ship for. To me, everything seemed fuzzy, and I couldn't even think straight. I wondered if space travel did that to everyone.

We walked out of the room, Yash and Sarthak talking about something… dumb probably. Anu came to stand by me, and said, "Do you feel dizzy too?"

"Yeah," I said, and thought it must be a consequence of… something. Why couldn't I think properly?

CHAPTER 2

Gas Really be Exploding

PARI

I looked around the room and found Jammari, the scientist, who I had seen for quite a while in the dream-thingy. I had just assumed he was short, because he looked out of place. I didn't assume that the Marsians would be humongous people. Well, that sounded wrong.

The view outside was beautiful and terrifying. I didn't know why I kept going back to the view. It was like I couldn't think properly. I guess space travel does have its consequences. I tried to focus on different things so that I couldn't think about the view again.

"Why," Sarthak panted, "Are we so dizzy?"

I raised my eyebrows. "And I would know?" I couldn't complete my sentence.

"It was a rhetorical question, you dum-dum."

Anu and Yash turned to look at him and simultaneously said, "Huh?" All of us were talking goofy.

I was trying so hard not to laugh, and I could see that all the people that came from Earth were like this. Clove's parents looked overwhelmed.

Sarthak nudged me and said, "If someone had a stroke right now, I wouldn't be surprised."

I agreed with him.

"Dark," Gertrude said.

All of us were so giddy it was almost sad.

There was another distinct boom. The guy who had greeted Glenda when we had first seen the ships shouted at Jammari. "I thought you said the planet was gone."

"Well apparently not!" Jammari shouted back.

It took me a moment to realize what they were saying. The *Mizrom* stuff must be exploding again. That meant we had to get out of there fast, and we had just got here. We were also very close to the floating bits of planet, and I could see red and orange explosions on the surface. I laughed, and I was pretty sure that I would have done this if I was feeling normal too. I just laughed at our awesome luck. Sometimes hated myself.

The ship hummed, and there was another explosion, but I felt the tremors in the ship.

"The engines have gone down!" someone shouted.

Of all the things the debris could've hit, it chose the most crucial thing of our escape. I felt like crying and hitting someone at the same time. I also felt like laughing. Having so many mixed emotions was a first for me.

I silently thanked space travel or whatever made me dizzy.

Red lights blinked everywhere in the ship. The ship hummed again, probably them trying to start it up. When I thought about it, it was dumb. They were probably not trying to start it up.

Before we knew it, some people came in and announced that the engine was fixed, but the ship hummed again. The humming was really loud now, and it felt like something alive.

"Monster!" someone yelled. Something buzzed lightly in my ear. I touched and realized there was something in it. I started freaking out and pulled it out, but suddenly all I could hear was an alien language. I realized it was a translator and put it back in. I was listening to languages I could decipher now.

I realized that monster wasn't probably what they said, because while the translator was not in, I heard a lot of something that sounded like *Baraak*, which, if I used my brain, probably meant monster in the Marsians' language. It was… a monster named monster?

People operating the ship were moving about frantically. There was a growl and a blast that I assumed was from some gun. The growl shook the whole ship. The thing had to be massive to do that. Everybody looked pretty scared. Glenda and Gertrude were near us too.

The ship still glowed red, but I was pretty sure the engines were fixed, yet the ship didn't move.

"Why isn't the ship moving?" Sarthak asked Glenda.

"We're facing the planet, and they're having difficulty turning. If we move, we'll run into the planet."

Explosions from the planet occasionally rocked our ship now and then.

"How much does this thing weigh?" Yash asked Glenda.

"I don't know exactly, but I would imagine its heavy." She laughed. "I think it's like 2000 kilotons."

Yash scoffed. "That's insane."

"Agreed."

The *Baraak* groaned like it had been eating too much again. This thing loved its groans.

We felt the hum of the engines that were firing up, but we still didn't move. There was an announcement from the speakers that we should get out of the door on the left. Since there was only one door, I didn't see how that made sense. As we went out, I saw something slimy moving outside the potholes. It seemed like a lot of other people did too, and we rushed outside the door into… another, identical room.

But the room suddenly started slowly rotating, but we still didn't move. Looks of confusion ran around in the people who were from Earth. I guess the Marsians who did these kinda things were pretty used to it. I wasn't dizzy now and didn't feel like falling over.

There was a *very* loud groan again. What was this guy's problem? Did he *want* me to go kick his eyes out? The ship suddenly shook, and the engine fired up properly this time. Seats popped out of the ground, next to every person. I wondered how that worked too. I sat and a seatbelt popped out and wrapped itself around me. I sat back in my seat because – well, what else could I do?

I saw as our ship speeded into space that slimy bits and pieces were on our windows. *Gross,* I grimaced. Sarthak nearly gagged. He had a bad reaction to gore, one that had been hilarious to see when we were watching *The Boys.*

Yash had his hand on his chin. "I don't think that thing is off yet."

"Why not?"

"No loud groan."

His explanation was so bizarre it was almost believable. But the soldiers (if that was what they were) nodded in agreement with Yash. They told us that the *Baraak* was still on the ship, and they had moved us to this room so that we weren't in danger of being squeezed.

Our view outside was completely blocked now by slimy bits and pieces. There were no lights of stars or planets far away anymore. We gained more speed as we went on, and a nasty smell of something *burning* wafted in. I was pretty sure the Marsians/*Nameri* didn't use rubber on their ships.

I sniffed in disgust. The ship lurched as the speed increased, and the smell intensified. I was pretty sure the *Baraak* didn't have a brain. Or maybe it was just hitching a ride to terrify some other ship.

The ship started frickin shaking left and right, reminding me of scenes where cars or planes tried to shake someone or something off, which made me laugh for some reason. The people in the ship were surprisingly not in a panic when the ship suddenly started waving about like a flag in the wind. I wondered what kind of hell these people had gone through to remain unruffled by our wet-dog-like ship.

The ship abruptly stopped. Abruptly was an over statement, since everybody would be a permanent smudge on the walls if it suddenly hit brakes. It came to a stop in a couple seconds was better.

Everybody's seatbelts made clicking noises. I almost didn't feel anything, because of the padding on my seatbelt. I still felt like throwing up.

Meanwhile the ship was dead silent, and I thought I could hear somet*hing* moving, making lots of weird slimy noises. Could noises be slimy? It was the *Baraak*, and like all stereotypical large and dangerous monsters, had a large amount of goo and slime around and on it and made squelchy noises.

"This is so cliché," I scoffed. "I didn't think real life monsters would be squelchy."

"Please stop talking," Sarthak groaned.

"I mean, think about all the generic things we've been through. This is lazy writing."

"Are you drunk?" Anu looked at me weird. "But I agree."

I cursed at her.

Everybody else in the ship was dead silent, as if waiting for something. The General walked in. He looked at Glenda and Jammari and both of them immediately got up. They walked out of the room together.

Slowly but surely, the silence started to break, people looking over each other's shoulders to talk to each other. Clove and her parents were still disoriented. I had forgotten she was even here. How long had it been since we had decided to go on that goddamn cycling picnic? What were we even thinking? Why did the four of us and our parents think it was a good idea to let four teenagers go on this damn trip?

But the fact that these guys were able to evacuate a planet in the time I took getting ready for school but couldn't shake off a snake worm really baffled me.

I wondered what Glenda was doing. She had gone with the General, which was a weird thing to have as a name, and Jammari. (Not that the name 'Jammari' wasn't weird to me, but it may or may not have been weird on *his* planet. Wait – Jammari was from *our* planet. I kept forgetting that both of us were earth… people.)

As soon as I finished thinking about Glenda, of course Glenda entered the room.

Seatbelts popped out of some of the seats again, and as soon as Jammari and the General were seated in the front, and Glenda came back to her place near Gertrude, we took off with a bang.

I was knocked into my seat yet again. This was getting boring. I realized that I was finding sitting calmly without any danger *boring*.

Wow.

But it was as if someone heard my call for danger and the ship started sputtering.

"We'll have to fight it!" someone said out loud.

People made collective incredulous noises. I didn't even know that was a thing up until now. People made collective noises?

I heard ships leaving our ship and guns all around us. I guess they were fighting it.

It went on for five minutes, literal noises of *pew pew*. I never thought I would hear Star Wars in real life. But it seemed to make no effect, because even after five minutes had gone by, the *Baraak* still hadn't moved, or for that matter, even groaned a single time.

Not that I was complaining.

I noticed that I could see through some of the portholes through the goo and slime. I saw that we were near Marsars again, and soon as I realized that there were *boom* noises. The ship started shaking, and a fire broke out somewhere. But the explosions were causing the *Baraak* to slip off the ship. I assumed they were bombs until I saw the planet. The planet was exploding even more.

How recent was this?

I looked at Glenda. "When did this planet start exploding?

"Yesterday."

"So… recent?" Sarthak said.

"I think it's safe to say yesterday is recent, dude," Yash replied.

He frowned but said nothing.

"There is no comeback to stupidity," Clove said to him, and patted him on the back.

He frowned harder but still said nothing. I almost saw him smirking, though.

The fire had been put out, but as I watched, more fires broke out and were put out. The way soldiers in general handled danger really made me marvel. Like even on earth, I was pretty sure that if space travel was normalized things like these would not even shake them a little bit. Or maybe they would cry for their mommies. Who knew what humanity was capable of.

The ship started bobbing a little.

The *Baraak* was off the ship.

We started speeding away from Marsars. Everything turned to a black and blue blur outside the window. We stopped in… space.

Lights turned red again.

"Get to the escape pods!" someone yelled, and we followed Jammari into yet another room. This one was small and had many doors. Clove and her parents went with Glenda, while we were with Gertrude.

"It's probably Hanginton, right?" Yash said.

"Most probably, yeah," Sarthak said.

How did she find ways to come after people so quickly? I was pretty sure she was after Glenda and Gertrude, and a lot of important Marsian people. Maybe us too, but I didn't think we were priority right about now. She wanted to cripple the Marsians by possibly killing The General and Jammari. We may have stopped some of her plans, but we couldn't do much on a bigger scale. We couldn't stop her by ourselves, that's why she was so focused on taking out the big… people? We did stop a pretty serious operation kind of by ourselves so there was that.

We got into the seats and for once, the seatbelts were normal. After a moment, we speeded away.

"Where are we going?" Anu said to Gertrude.

"How would I know?" Gertrude said, giving Anu an incredulous look.

"I don't know. Why would I know that you don't know?" Anu said.

Gertrude made some confused noises and decided to give up, making Anu the victor of that useless banter. It was things like these that made me like Anu a lot. It was just… wholesome. I cringed at the thought.

After a moment, we stopped speeding through space. I saw that we were back to earth, and near the south pole. That probably meant we were going to meet the *Namerians*, the people who had decided to side with the Marsians, and the twins of the *Whizari*. I mean we were kinda escaping something/someone, but we were still gonna meet them.

We were near a desolate wasteland. There was nothing around us. That is until I felt an electric *zing* and suddenly a city appeared to us. It was breathtakingly beautiful. It was kinda similar to *H'vannat*, but they were obviously different, even though they were basically in the same era, but as it was in every different place, their cultures varied.

It was visible in the way their buildings were built. *H'vannat* was built more, like, *standard*. *Nameri*, the *Namerians* city, however, was much more chaotic. The way the pods functioned, and the way roads and airways were marked, figured for a much more chaotic city than *H'vannat*. Roadways zigzagged through large buildings, train tracks went through big skyscrapers, insinuating that they were built *around* the tracks, which was bizarre.

We landed at the edge of the city, in what looked to me like a military base. Several other ships were landing here too but compared to what ships were already resting in the base, they were nothing. *Namerian* and Marsian technology put side by side made the Marsian ones look so pathetic. Not even their functionality. They just looked… *clean.*

I realized I hadn't seen how the room inside the aircraft was, or for that matter had a plate of doughnuts on a table. How did I miss these doughnuts?

There was a hiss and a door opened. We unbuckled our seatbelts and went to stand outside, where we met Glenda and Clove and her parents. I realized that from a group of four to a group of seven we had gone up to a group of 10. There were also Mrs. Pandit and Shubham and Kartik, who had to leave because of their mother injuring herself. It seemed like it had happened a year ago but was actually only a week. So much had happened. I remembered the hide-and-seek in the maze. It was almost nostalgic, and I had to remind myself that it had been like 10-12 days ago. I shook my head.

The General came over from his ship. He was a very tall guy, and mysterious. He had neon yellow eyes like a cat, and I realized that every Marsian's eye glowed in the pitch darkness. The fact that our only difference in looks were cat-like eyes was funny. I was pretty sure that if I said light-bulb eyes to any Marsian I would get yeeted off a ship while we were in space.

A man came from the base surrounded by a lot of security people with *batons* of all weapons they could have. Well, they were probably batons that could shoot lasers and turn into a gun if needed.

Who was I to say?

"Hello, Glenda," the man said, "General," he nodded. "Grumpy as usual, I see."

I sensed corny dad jokes about to emanate from the midst of their meeting, since they seemed to be good friends.

"It's not like my planet exploded or anything." He slapped the man on the shoulder, and they hugged.

"But you're still sulking like every day. I bet that you won't even smile when someone cracks a good joke." I almost physically cringed at that.

The General smiled. "My friend, I have never smiled at you."

There were some awkward giggles.

"No one has ever cracked me," Tobias said.

"Ah yes," the man said. "Let me just introduce myself after this embarrassment. I'm Tobias. I'm the, well, advisor/husband of the head of this city. She had a runny nose and unfortunately couldn't come."

"So advanced and y'all yet haven't made a common cold insta-cure," Jammari tutted.

They had the energy of teenagers. It was really funny.

"Why do you have names of a person from the US?" Yash said to Tobias.

"Oh, we have names from all over the Earth. My wife's name is Selena."

"Our culture decided to have different names, and not like the ones you have," Jammari said. "It kinda sucks that we have names that sound like diseases."

"Your name is…" Anu tried to say something. "It sounds like a disease."

"See? Even newbies know that it sucks. It was one of the reasons I left them." Jammari raised his hands at the incredulous looks we gave him. "Chill, I was joking."

I was already liking these people, and I had just met them.

CHAPTER 3

The Edge

PARI

I wondered what we were going to do now. I didn't think that we could leave this city without getting killed by Hanginton. Striker had been brought to us in a box. He jumped all over Sarthak. I felt bad for the poor dog.

"So, what do we do now?" Getrude said to Glenda.

"Sleep," Glenda said. I looked at my phone and realized it was very late, according to Greenland time. I kept forgetting when I was supposed to sleep, because we were travelling so much. At this point I just slept whenever I was tired. And hadn't I slept in the ship? Why was I still so tired?

"Yay," Clove yawned.

We *were* tired. Well, considering all we had gone through, this was called for.

We arrived in our rooms. They were like normal rooms, with beds and tables and lamps. The four of us were sharing a room. It had two beds. I basically jumped on one and was out. I didn't even see the room.

When I woke up, Sarthak, Anu and Yash were still asleep. I wasn't feeling sleepy now. I went over to a window and opened the curtains. The view was breath-taking.

Snow fell into the city, coating the buildings, which were *tall*. The city lights were like normal cities, and I could see pods flying through the air in lines. I could see the lanes in the air, and it looked like people had just begun their day, because a lot of them were walking, and not many pods were there.

I took out my phone and hoped that they had Wi-Fi without a password. Fortunately, they did. I decided to check the speed and it was about 1 GBPS. So, I did what I could do.

I scrolled.

After about half an hour, Anu woke up. Her hair, as always, was perfect. I was pretty sure it would be perfect even if she travelled through the whole Sahara Desert or something at this point.

She ruffled them and came over to the sofa I was sitting on and began eating, of all things, *muffins* from her backpack. The muffins we had bought about 2 weeks ago.

"Don't they smell?" I said to her.

"A little," she said. "But it's okay."

"Eating an item that expired a week ago, is okay? Are *you* okay?"

"Maybe," she yawned. "But I don't know."

"You got problems."

"I know."

Sarthak woke up. When I say *woke up,* I mean opened his eyes, even thought he was in the bed flopping around for five minutes until I threw a pillow at him. Then he moved around and came over to us and casually pushed Anu out of the spot on the couch. She pushed him back and sent him flying into Yash, who woke up with a gasp.

"What's wrong with you?" Yash and Sarthak said at the same time.

"I don't know," Anu said. She got weird looks from the three of us.

"I'm sleepy," she protested.

"So… you're always sleepy?" I said to her.

She frowned and looked like she wanted to hit me, but we were interrupted by Gertrude, who came in, looked at us and said, "Sleepyheads."

"Thanks, boomer," Yash said.

Gertrude huffed but said nothing about it. "Go in the bathrooms and take a shower. We're gonna take a city tour since there is nothing else we can do."

I got my towel from my bag, Striker sleeping near it. I rubbed his head and went into the bathroom.

I spent the next hour in there, entertaining myself with all of the different options I could shower with. It also helped that there was a tub. When I came out, Sarthak was still in, but Yash and Anu looked like they had been out for a long time, because Anu's hair was dry, and Yash was on his phone.

When all of us were ready I went out of my room and found myself in a lobby with four rooms. I assumed the five rooms were for us, Clove and her parents, Glenda, Gertrude and Hamilton.

Wait – *where was Hamilton?*

"Where's Hamilton?" I said to Getrude as soon as I saw her.

"Back home in Greenland. He had to leave because he had to do something," she replied.

"What thing?" Yash said.

"You don't need to know that."

"We sure don't but we *want* to," Sarthak said.

"Then I don't wanna tell you." Glenda huffed. "It's related to the Hangintons. He hasn't even told me what it was."

"So why were you pretending you knew what it was?" Yash said and grinned. "It's ok. Everyone needs a sense of importance. We're not gonna judge you."

Glenda said nothing. I had feeling she knew, but wasn't telling us, probably because Hamilton had asked her to. I wondered what he could be doing. And wasn't what we were already doing related to the Hangintons? Stopping one from trying to take over the world? Wasn't that also related to the Hangintons? It must be some other thing, and I decided to leave it.

I had a city tour to look forward to.

I was wearing jeans and a blue T-Shirt, since I could tell that this was not going to be cold. When we went out of the building, we met up with Glenda and Clove. Clove's parents were in their rooms, apparently too overwhelmed.

"They're old," Clove said.

She was looking around the city with a glint in her eyes. I suddenly realized why – she hadn't been outside a room in a long, *long* time. If someone looked at her, no one would ever realize that about her.

"How're you feeling?" I said to her.

"Well," she said. "Overwhelmed."

I kept my arm on her shoulder. "Everyone is," I smiled.

"Who knew you could be nice?" Sarthak said. To my surprise, Anu punched him. She was usually the one who proceeded to make fun of me after I was made fun of.

"News to me," Yash muttered.

Before we could continue, we got to the military base we were at yesterday, and we met Tobias and a tall woman, who must be Selena, his wife. She held herself like a queen and nodded at Glenda when she saw her. I saw that there were a lot of people around Tobias and the head of the city, probably security. I wondered what they needed to be protected from, but I guess every perfect thing has its own problems, making it *not* perfect. Which just went on to say that even technologically advanced cities like these are not perfect, and they never will be. I decided to stop thinking on that train of thought before I got all moody and serious. *14-year-old thinks solemn: nothing is perfect* did not sound like a good obituary.

"I'm Selena," said Selena. "Nice to meet you."

"You too," said Yash, and many greetings followed that. We started moving towards a vehicle, a *military* one, which made me think that this wasn't a standard city tour. We were probably gonna find out a lot more things other than how the city looked, but in the back of my mind, that wasn't what I was expecting anyway.

We got into the ship. It had many seats, and for some reason, a bottle of coke next to every seat. We took no time in draining out the cokes into glasses and gulping them down. The seats were padded and it looked like a normal bus, that is until it suddenly rose up in the air and before I knew it, we were about 200 metres up in the air. Since we were on the edge of the city, we couldn't really see much, but I could still see the silhouettes of the city buildings, which were I couldn't tell how tall.

"These buildings are *long*," Anu said.

"How sleepy are you?" Sarthak said.

When Anu looked at him in confusion, he said, "Buildings aren't long. My fingers are long."

"Same thing," she muttered. I wondered why she was pissed about something. I also wondered what things she could have to *be* pissed at.

I decided to ask her later. I saw that we weren't moving towards the city and rather *outwards*. I wondered what we were going to, and if it possibly was something related to Hanginton.

"We are over what we call 'The Edge'," said Selena.

It definitely looked like an edge, because it was all water after some land. I wondered why it was important.

"We saw traces of magic here," she continued.

I wondered what we had to do with them spotting magic outside their cities.

"We need your help," she said. "We need someone who is not from our city to go there."

All of us looked around at each other, dumbfounded.

"How does that matter?" Glenda said.

"Our people can't go in because of a certain gene in us."

"That makes no sense," Glenda said. "We're literally from the same planet."

"Ahh, but we aren't. Not many people know this, but we actually came from another planet many years ago, and those people had *magic* in them. Their genes, I mean. And the area we want to go into is blocked off to that *particular* kind of magic, and we want to find out why."

This sounded like a lot of random stuff, but it… made sense in a weird way.

"And… no adults from earth can go in."

Okay this was getting ridiculous. It was almost like the universe wanted us to risk our butts over some random things. But I also wanted to do it, so there was that too.

"Will it be very dangerous?" Sarthak said.

"No," Selena said. Before she could say anything else, she was interrupted.

"Whoa, whoa, whoa, wait," Glenda said. "You are *not* going there."

"It won't be dangerous," Selena said. "We're going to give you everything and tell you what you need to know. You're literally gonna be invisible, unless you decide to take off the helmet, which I highly recommend you don't do. All you need to do is get some information."

"What information?" Gertrude said.

"What kinda magic they're performing, and if we need to shut them down. They also set up here without telling us, which is very fishy."

"I'm down," Anu said. She received confirmation from each of us, including Clove.

"But why no adults?" Sarthak asked.

"No adults from *earth*," Selena replied.

"How does that work?" Yash said.

"We don't know."

"How *did* you come to know?" Glenda said.

Selena looked annoyed, so Tobias answered instead of her. "We tested it."

"How do you test… *that*?" Anu asked.

"Magic, a lot of the times, has age restrictions. So based on that theory, we sent a 16-year-old to try and enter it and it worked."

"When do we need to leave?" Yash said.

"Right now."

Sounded about right. I was excited to be in some action, which told a lot about how crazy I was going. Adrenaline rushed my body.

"We are sending you because nobody else your age from Earth knows all of this," Selena said. "And this may also be related to Soundleek Hanginton and the upcoming war of the Marsians and the *Whizari*."

She said upcoming war like it was a sequel to a popular movie franchise. I realized how normalized war was to these people, and it wasn't even with the people of their planet. It was like frickin Star Wars for them. I still hadn't seen any Light Sabers, but I hadn't yet counted that possibility out.

Someone came up from the front of the bus by opening a door and kept five helmets on the table in the corner. I assumed that they were the invisibility helmets Selena was earlier talking about. They looked really cool, with antenna-type thingys sticking out at the sides, and they were black. There was no way you could see out of the helmet, but I guessed that in an invisibility helmet, glass was of no use and would probably interrupt the process.

"How does this work?" I asked.

"They deposit micro-flakes on your body. Then these flakes mirror the surroundings," Tobias said. "It is very similar to the *Whizari* Cloak. Except that they have the whole cloak. It is very impressive, I must say."

It was funny how different these people were yet they had basically the same technologies.

"So how do we get out of here without freezing to death?" Yash asked.

"Clothes, idiot," Anu said.

"True," Tobias agreed with Yash.

Some white woollen-type clothes were brought, but they weren't thick enough to be proper woollen. When we started to wear them, they started to adjust around us. It was probably Nano-tech and sensors. They were very comfortable, and surprisingly, I was not hot.

"They adjust themselves according to the weather," someone said. The person who had handed us the clothes. "So, you'll be alright even if you land in lava."

I smirked. "We can fall in lava? It's that dangerous?" I looked over at Sarthak. "Shiver me timbers then."

"Yup," Tobias confirmed.

When the doors to the bus started to open, I realized we were not moving anymore. We were hovering over what I assumed was The Edge. All of us took the helmets and put them on. We weren't invisible yet, but I assumed it could be turned on or off. The helmet wasn't heavy at all; it was like I didn't even feel it.

"The drones will carry you down," I heard Tobias's yell over the wind. "You can activate the helmets by *thinking* yes. They are cybernetic. Your partners' helmets will be visible to you. Good luck!"

Drones came out of nowhere and clasped themselves onto our shoulders. I was lifted off my feet and we went – no, *dropped* – to The Edge so quickly my heart landed in my throat. In about 5 seconds time, we hit metal, and I saw that we were in a long tunnel. The drones silently ascended back to the bus.

Our helmets were activated automatically, probably from the bus. Someone spoke in my ear, making us all jump, which meant that all of us were hearing it.

"I forgot to tell you about the headset and the map on these things," Selena said. A map appeared on my screen, and on it a red dot. I saw that this place was a mess of lobbies and passages. But in the centre, there was just a blank space, just plain black.

"The black part is the magic-restricted part, and our technology can't detect it as well," Selena continued. "You just need to go to the red dot however you can, and then you just need to signal us. Drones will emerge from the helmets, but make sure you are alone right then, because you will be invisible for the duration of about a minute. There are Blasters in your right pockets, if you get into trouble. These passages are a piece of cake, and these headsets have very small batteries, so I won't be talking to you for that duration. All you need to do is think about it and I'll be available to you. Good luck."

All of us were silent for a moment.

Suddenly a voice spoke in our ear. *Go straight then go left.* And we had a personal GPS.

Nice.

We followed the GPS's directions for some time, and then the GPS stopped at a huge door. We had met no one during the travel through the large, dank hallways. I never got what the point of these hallways was. Were they sewers at some point? Why were they always there in places like these?

"So… we go through these?" Sarthak said.

"I think," said Clove. "But how?"

As soon as she said it, we heard voices. We all ducked into a corner.

"It's not necessary," Anu whispered. "We're invisible."

"We can see each other," I whispered back.

Yash took the opportunity of the comeback. "Thanks, Captain Obvious."

All of us got out of the corner. It was weird not seeing people and red highlights of floating helmets. There were two people, and I couldn't see their faces. They touched the doors and the doors opened. We followed them inside and found ourselves in a *massive* dome. Looking at our tiny figures on the map, I realized that this huge dome-type thing was probably the whole black thing.

The whole thing was open. It was fully blue. There were people all around, and we sure didn't expect this many of them to be here. All of them wore cloaks that covered their faces. They were about the height of every average Marsian. They were also built like them, and I saw people's eyes glowed like the Marsians' did.

"Are these Marsians?" Yash said.

"I don't think they are, no," Anu said. "The Marsians told us about *Xinains*, remember? That they kicked them off the planet. And the *Namerians* are allies to the Marsians. They must be plotting something against them."

"Your theory sounds like a conspiracy theory on Facebook," Clove said. "But it seems likely right about now."

"Hold up," Sarthak said. "How is this… *thing* here and the *Namerians* didn't notice this? How strong is this magic?"

"We don't need to know that right now," Yash said. "We need to contact the *Namerians*."

When we tried to do what Selena had said, it didn't work. I also noticed one thing. Nobody was using technology in here. They had put magic here so that it blocked all technology. But that also meant –

Our helmets started going haywire. It electrocuted itself off my head, leaving me exposed. My head was hurting a lot, and I couldn't even see straight now. I saw around me that my friends were also falling down on the floor. People could see us now. There were many shouts, and a moment later I saw the world hazing out. And I passed out.

When we woke up, we were on chairs. I was apparently the last one to wake up, and I still couldn't see properly. My head was aching. When I tried to bring my hands up to ease it, I found I couldn't move my hands. Some mysterious force had bound my hands to the chair. When I checked properly that mysterious force turned out to be a chain.

I couldn't think straight. I started to panic. I was having a panic attack after a long time. Suddenly the chains fell off. I fell down on the floor and grabbed my head. Sarthak rushed to me – I thought it was Sarthak – and sat me down on the chair, rubbing my temples.

"Breathe," he comforted me. "Take deep breathes. We're safe. Relax."

I slowly started to calm down, even though my headache wasn't improving. He kept rubbing my temples. The headache slowly receded, and I could see properly now. I looked around the room and saw that it was bare grey, but there were no cameras. Of course. No technology.

"How did you-?" I took a deep breath. "How did you get out?"

"Anu managed to do it. She had the gun in her frickin' sleeve when we fainted."

Clove was still passed out, and Yash was pacing around in the room. Anu was sitting on her chair, blaster in her hand. She was looking toward something I realized was the door, poised to take down anyone who might come.

Our helmets were in a corner. I went towards them and put one on to test it. It was working.

"It's working," Sarthak said. "We can get out. We just need a way to break this door."

"Wait," Yash said, pausing his pacing. "If we get out of here, our helmets will stop working."

"They probably won't," Anu said. "Because we *are* at the red dot. All we need to do is deploy the drones. For now, I mean."

"Yes," Clove said. "Get your helmets and put them on."

We did and the drones emerged. The drones were about the size of my hand, and they flew over to a corner in the wall and started to cut lasers in them. They flew out and our headsets were suddenly activated.

"You guys, okay?"

It was Selena's voice. I sighed with relief.

"Yes, except for the fact that we have been captured," Yash said.

"What am I seeing?" Tobias's voice came from the background.

"What *is* this?" Gertrude said.

"It's a portal. From *Xin*." Selena said. "I need to call the General, but first we have to get you out of there. We are sending a ship down there. There is a vent that leads to near wherever you are, and it will blow its path through to you. But you need to move fast after it comes to you."

"Ok. We're waiting," I replied. "But wait. What about the information?"

"You need to get out of there alive. We can find another way."

Before we could talk more, the door opened and a woman came in. She looked at us and was silenced by Anu, who was still poised with the blaster in hand. The woman fainted on the spot, and we closed the door behind her. There were shouts outside, and we could hear people rushing towards us. Outside the door. The door opened, and whoever tried to came in was stopped by our barrage of lasers from our blasters, but only for a few seconds. There was a purple release of energy and suddenly all of us were floating in the air.

We were now suspended in the air. A tall woman came in through the door, and she had purple bands of writhing energy moving around her. She had black hair and black eyes. She was kinda wrinkly and had the look of a middle-aged woman. She was wearing purple robes, and gave me full evil-magic vibes. When I had imagined evil-magic, I had not imagined it to be this scary.

But we were only suspended for about ten seconds, before we fell back to ground, because of a nearby explosion.

The ship was here.

All of us shot at the woman, and she took a step back, allowing us mere seconds to get to the hole our ship had caused. We kept shooting her, and as soon as all of us were in the ship, the door closed and we started moving. But half a second later, the ship got stopped in its path, and fire broke out in it. The door opened and we were thrown out, shaking like ragdolls. The woman had purple bands around her again.

"Stay where you are!" she said, and it sounded like several voices were speaking at once. "Try to move, and you die!"

We took the hint this time, and we flopped to the ground. The woman came into the room and looked at us.

"You're not worth killing," she said. "We could use you."

Anu tried to shoot her once. The shot stopped in mid-air. All of us were lifted into the air, and smashed into the wall. I blacked out, along with everyone.

CHAPTER 4

Amnesia

ANU

I was about to end my shift. It had been a long day, what with many problems in the lab and the people coming through. I had to deal with a lot of things like cleaning up the explosion and accommodating new people coming through. Me and my friend Pari had speculated that the *Xinains* were moving to the compound, and maybe what was outside. We had never been allowed to go out, and my curiosity always bugged me.

I met up with Pari and two of my friends, Yash and Sarthak.

"How were your shifts?" Sarthak asked.

"Like always," Pari replied.

Sarthak and I looked very similar. I sometimes wondered that when we were created in the labs, they had used the same genes for me and him. Pari looked kind of like us too. We went to our separate rooms and went to sleep.

The next morning, we woke up and surprisingly, the four of us had a duty together. We got the information from bands on our arms. It was very efficient.

After our duty, we went to my room to sit down. I always had a nagging feeling that I had been in the world outside.

"Let's go outside," I said to my friends.

"Are you crazy?" Pari said. 'Do you wanna die?"

"I found these clothes," I said. They were white clothes, and when I had worn them, they adjusted around me, which I found really intriguing. I told them about it, and I took them over to my closet. The clothes were in there.

"But how do we get out with these clothes on?" Sarthak said.

"We can pose as one of the workers, who go outside every day. It will be quite easy," I said.

As we were talking about it, there was an explosion above us. We covered our heads. There were many shouts from outside our room. We looked at each other in fear, and started to run out, but a gaping hole appeared above us, and a beam came down and captured us. We shouted, and we fainted.

When we woke up, we were surrounded by machines. There were some bowl-type thingys on our heads, and we were surrounded by people who seemed oddly familiar. When we tried to speak, I realized that there were some clasps on our mouths.

We were in there for five minutes when my memories came back.

We were surrounded by Glenda, Gertrude and Clove. Selena and Tobias were there in the back too. All of us kind of woke up with a gasp, overwhelmed with the flood of memories. Clove, I noticed, had cut her red hair shorter. I wondered how long it had been. I also noticed that we weren't in the same bus we had come in.

"How long…?" I asked. "How long has it been?"

"10 months," Clove said.

I almost gagged. "What?!"

Glenda smacked Clove. "It's been a week."

I sighed in relief and kicked Clove in the shin.

"Why did you cut your hair?" Pari asked.

"It got damaged when the ship exploded. Another ship was sent and I luckily got out of there. But y'all weren't so lucky," she cast a glance towards her parents and said, "I wanted to get my hair coloured too. They didn't let me."

I nodded and said, "Unfortunate."

"*Unfortunate*," she mimicked my voice badly.

"At least we survived," Sarthak said. "And it wasn't a year." He frowned.

"Sorry about that," Clove said sheepishly.

"We found out a lot of things about them. So, it wasn't a complete failure," Gertrude said. 'And nobody died too, so there's that."

"Yeah, what a positive," Pari said. "Nobody died."

"Don't ever say what a positive again," I said. "It makes you sound like a preschool teacher."

But I was still thinking. Why did they wipe us? Why not kill us instead? I remembered the scary woman wreathed in purple. We had people like these to deal with. I suddenly felt genuinely scared for the first time in this adventure. The thought that we could die with a single *command* scared the crap out of me.

"Why did they memory wipe us?" I asked Gertrude. "Why not kill us?"

"Yeah," Sarthak said. "We were told we're not worth killing. I think I'm a very worthy candidate."

Before we could talk further, we heard whirring noises outside. Before we knew it, we were surrounded by ships.

"Give our prisoners back to us," a voice resounded in our ship. Didn't they know slaves were illegal?

We speeded away towards *Nameri*, and in a few split seconds, we were in the city, and I didn't even feel a jerk. I wondered how that worked. How did they bend physics? I wondered if they used magic for this too. They probably did.

I felt the same electric zing I had felt when we had first entered *Nameri*. We were in the city, and I saw through the windows that a force-field rose behind us. It looked as if they were prepared for attack. It amazed me how quickly they could do that. They were so quick in everything, and it didn't just mean tech. It meant organising things. It meant coordination.

We got out at the military base, and were led into the building. It had people in a frantic hurry, rushing to their duties. It was chaos. Outside the force field, many ships were emerging, but they were getting shot out of the sky, because of the anti-artillery guns all over it. It was very loud, what with gunshots and bangs.

"So…" Gertrude said. "What do we do?"

"We sit, and wait for our troops to destroy their base," Selena said. She didn't look worried at all, which told me how much faith she had in her city's defences. It may seem like over-confidence, but with how quick the ships of the *Xinains* were being destroyed and how the explosions were being blocked made me think that her confidence was well justified.

I saw massive ships rise up in the air, and there was a massive *BANG* as all the ships collectively exploded. I could feel that the *Xinains* base was about to be destroyed. I saw Selena holding a tablet, and saw on her screen that a ship was going to The Edge.

The ship started scanning something, but…

"The base is not there anymore," Selena said. "This was a decoy for them to get out. The base disappeared."

I wondered how that big of a base just *disappears*. My guess was TechnoMagic. A mixture of Nano-Tech and really, *really* strong magic.

"This doesn't seem ri-" Glenda started to say, but glass rained down from above us, and people scrambled around to dodge it. I wondered how that happened. I saw that there was a *Xinain* ship hovering above us, and it was destroyed in a split second.

"Where did that come from?" The General and Jammari were here.

"Underground," Selena said. "It tore through our defences underground. Activate the *Silvet*!" I assumed that the *Silvet* was probably their main defence for the city.

And it was.

A screen emerged out of nowhere in the base, and we looked towards it. There was a massive pyramid floating in the air, and it was shooting literal thunderbolts towards the ships. Hundreds and hundreds of thunder bolts appeared and destroyed the ships around it. It looked marvellous, and at the same time very scary. It was outside the force field, and before we knew it, all of the ships were destroyed.

And then the *Silvet* burst in pieces, due to a huge laser coming out of nowhere and obliterating it. But it started to rebuild, and even as it was rebuilding, it destroyed ships.

It was then that we saw the hologram of Soundleek Hanginton.

"Hello, *Namerians*," it said. That was all it could say before it was destroyed by the *Silvet*. At least we didn't have to put up with her nonsense for now. I also felt angry that this woman was not leaving us. A ship crashed into the base, and luckily landed on the massive fountain in the middle, drenching us all. From that ship emerged hundreds of people, and behind them all, Soundleek Hanginton came.

I wanted to kick Hanginton so hard right now.

The people with her shot everyone they saw, killing no one. I wondered why Hanginton cared enough to do that. She may as well do it. I was pretty sure it wouldn't affect her.

Drones flew over to us with speed, and the four of us, Selena, Tobias, Clove, Glenda, Gertrude, The General and Jammari were clasped in handcuffs. Right now, we were the only ones not down on the floor.

"So, we meet again," Hanginton said. "I always wanted to kill you myself."

"You failed though," Sarthak said, and as soon as he did, there was a thunderbolt, right next to Hanginton, throwing her into the wall. Many more people were thrown into the walls, but with the force Hanginton was thrown into the wall – she had to be dead. There was no way Sarthak knew that was coming, but his timing felt like something out of a movie.

Many ships came through the wall, and tased the people that were not knocked out. We rushed to Hanginton, saw some blood on her face... and realized she was dead.

"It's over?" Pari said. "Like that?"

"Yes," Glenda said.

"Huh."

CHAPTER 5

Recalling
An Year Later

ANU

Our school had ended a week ago. I mean, not school, but our vacations started today. It was a normal, boring day at school.

It was May. It had almost been one year since Hanginton was killed, which had been kinda anti-climactic. I was happy that we got to go home, though. We had rescued my parents, and I was living with them. We still lived in the same place, and Yash's parents had decided to move back to India, so that was a plus. But some connection with my parents was also shredded, since they didn't tell us about their history with the Tiaras, the rivals of the Hangintons, and that I was frickin adopted.

I spent a lot more time with Sarthak and Pari now. It was kinda bizarre that they were my literal brother and sister, and Sarthak was my twin. I didn't really still think of them like that. They were still my friends, and I was pretty sure they didn't think of me like that too.

It had always been weird that we had landed right in the middle of a coincidence. It somehow seemed planned, and for some reason I didn't put it past our parents to set that up. I had mustered up the courage to ask my parents, and felt really bad afterwards, but I still believed they could have done this.

There was a lot to do in our summer vacations before we had the adventure. I kinda craved for that again now. Not risking my life, but for excitement. School had never been *not* boring, so I didn't have a problem with school. I didn't really have a *problem* with anything, but I just felt… empty. Like I didn't have purpose in life, which was really stupid, since the adventure we had had only been two weeks.

"Hey," Pari said. She was smiling. Sarthak was behind her. "Whatcha doin'?"

"Having an existential crisis," I said.

"Yeah, we do it sometimes too," Sarthak said. "Everybody does that, right?"

I kicked him in the groin with my knee, and he shut up.

"Yash was coming over, right?" Pari said. "What're we doing?"

"I don't know. Let's go out to eat or something," I said.

As we were talking about him, the bell rang and Yash came in. All of us were taller by at least 3 or 4 inches since last year, but Yash had *grown*. He was about 5 feet 11 inches now. He was almost 7 inches taller than me, and 4 inches taller than Pari, who was taller than Sarthak, who wasn't much happy about that.

We went out to a place that made awesome sandwiches, went to Starbucks to get coffee (Yes there was one in Indore), and started to go to our homes when we fell through a hole in the footpath. A hole in the frickin footpath.

We landed on cushion-y stuff. It was fully dark. After a moment, the lights turned on.

And the General emerged from the darkness. We hadn't seen him since last year, and I didn't think I ever would. We had met Gertrude, and we had met Glenda, because they were kinda well known to our parents. But I had never ever thought that I would get to meet *him* again, and I was pretty sure he was here for our help, though I wondered what 4 14-year-olds could do about anything he said.

"Long time no see," he said, and I wondered who in the hell still said those words.

"How old are you?" Sarthak said.

He sighed. All of us laughed, not at all fazed by him appearing right out of nowhere. It was like we expected that. I wondered how just two weeks had changed us. And they were a year ago too. I guess that we thought about it every day, and that did tend to make a change in our thoughts and reactions.

"Why are you here?" Pari said.

"As you may have guessed, I need your help," he said.

I interrupted him. "If it has something to do with the *Xinain* magic, I'm out."

"I agree," Yash said. Sarthak and Pari nodded. All of us had been shook by that event a *lot*. I don't know why, because we had been in much dangerous situations, but there was a chance of us surviving. Like we didn't lose hope at that moment.

But I remember feeling absolutely helpless when we were detained by the woman in purple robes, the absolute fear of magic I had felt in those few moments, and fear for my life. Pari didn't feel much because she had suffered the most due to the helmet's injury. It was good, I think. But she had a lot of headaches nowadays. Damn that helmet. The rest of us had just had out helmets thrown off our heads, nothing major.

I randomly remembered Sarthak's injury on his arm, when he had burned it when we were trying to go in to stop the Strike on the Satellite. He had got hit by the Asphaltier, and should not have survived, but his arm was never the same again. His arm had been *very* strong, but now, it just couldn't handle some things now. He couldn't lift things that he could easily before, and all that. Both Sarthak and Pari had got injuries that would be with them their whole life. I was just afraid it was going to be me or Yash next.

"It is not that," the General said. "This one might be… kind of personal."

"Oh," Pari said, sounding relieved. It was just a favour. But I wondered why he was asking *us* again. "What do you want us to do?"

"I want you to infiltrate a place," he said.

"Where?" Pari said. "On Earth?"

"Yeah," he said.

"Good, because we aren't going anywhere else," Sarthak said. I think he spoke for all of us. I definitely did *not* wanna go to space one more time in my entire life, except if Elon Musk acted up and commercial space travel became easier. But who knows?

"I know that" the General said. "And I come to you because only people your age can do this."

"What is it?" I almost shouted, getting impatient. The damn guy was talking so long getting to the point. "A frickin school?

"No," the General said. "It's kind of a job."

"For teenagers?" Yash said. "Like a *job* job?

"Yes," the General said. "I know it's strange, but they want people of your age to participate in an experiment. You are to pose as some other kids."

I interrupted him again. "Will we be like spies? Because I don't like that."

He looked annoyed at all the interruptions, but I didn't care. "Yes, you kinda will be like spies. But you do not need to stop anyone. All you need to do is get information from in there."

"So, what *is* it?" Sarthak said.

"A Marsian space explorer wants teenagers to – what the-?" The General was interrupted as we heard something outside the room. Someone was banging… *something* on the door. Suddenly the door fell to pieces and Gertrude came through. She shot the General, and he literally *fell to pieces.*

This was not the real General.

"What the hell?" Yash exclaimed.

I was very unruffled, considering that we had just seen what could have been a man disappear. If it was an actual guy, he would've *died*.

"You're welcome," Gertrude sniffed. "I saved your lives. This Xinain bot was trying to capture people who have information about the Marsians and try to use it any way they can. The people of Xin are helping the Whizari fight the war, leaving more work for me."

That answered the unasked question of where she had been for some time. And I had almost forgotten about the war the Marsians were about to fight. I found out I couldn't give a damn what those two did.

"Well, thank you for saving our life, Gertrude," Sarthak said, trying to sound sincere but all of us burst laughing at that.

When we got out of the room, I realized that there had been a door the whole time.

"How did you find us?" I asked Gertrude.

She was taken aback. "Can I not meet you guys?" Me and my friends looked at each other. This was definitely a lie. We knew that Gertrude wasn't the type of person that just crashed a party for crashing a party. She had a lot of other reason besides that, possibly kidnapping someone or stopping a nuclear explosion.

It depended on the situation. Never knew with her.

"Yeah, ok," Yash said in fake agreement. Even Gertrude knew we knew that what she said was a blatant frickin lie. I decided to drop it, since we weren't gonna get an answer anyways.

"Let's get you home," she said. We got in her car to head to our home, but we decided to take a detour to the theatre because we were bored and none of us felt like going home. We watched the movie, which was about 2 hours long, and decided to eat at the theatre. It was about 9 or 10 by the time we get back. We dropped off Yash at his home, and after a moment, he called us.

"Guys," he sounded urgent. "Get here. Fast. My parents are not here, not picking up my call, and my house is in shambles. Unless they had a bad fight and threw their phones at the house objects, something bad has happened."

I wondered how he wasn't panicking out of his mind and could say all of that. We arrived at his house and went inside. The house was a mess. All of the couches were out of place. The TV was on the ground, probably shattered. I wondered how the people who kidnapped – which was probably what happened – Yash's parents had the guts to do it. How DARE they destroy the TV. It was a really nice T.V.

As soon as the door closed, we were ambushed by people. They had guns that looked like the Puke Gun. That was almost nostalgic.

I had a feeling that this was Hanginton. I knew that she had to be dead, but this was her. And the people had the same blue, red and black uniforms they were wearing when they had fought us in Greenland in Hamilton's house.

And then she emerged, wearing the same uniform as her henchmen.

"Guess who's alive," she said.

"Cringe," Yash murmured.

"What did you say?" she said.

"I said it was cringe, you idiot."

She huffed. "Maybe. But shut up." She turned to Gertrude. "You're the one I'm here for. You have so much stuff I want to know, and so much I don't want you *to* know."

Gertrude stood her ground and spat at Hanginton. "How are you even alive?"

"The body was a goddamn robot," Hanginton snarled, wiping her face. "We were prepared, unlike your coward friends in *Nameri*.

"Good bot," Gertrude mimed, raising an eyebrow. I could tell that she didn't believe it, and neither did we.

"You don't look afraid." Hanginton sounded disappointed.

None of us said anything. She was downright indignant that none of us was afraid of her. I wondered why we weren't dead already. Gertrude had her uses, but what about us?

On that cheerful note, the room filled with gas and we fainted on the spot.

CHAPTER 6

Space

ANU

My head hurt and I was groggy. I had not counted the number of times we had fainted on this goddamn thing. It may or may not have been more or less than 5.

I honestly had no idea.

Looking outside the window told me we were no longer on earth. Space was the last place I wanted to be. The room seemed to be inescapable, with no visible routes or doors for helping us escape. A bland shade of blue on the walls was the only thing that made this room kinda humane. There were footsteps that resounded in the medium-sized room though. My vision cleared a little bit.

My friends were waking up at about the same time as me, and as the footsteps grew louder, I turned to its source.

Hanginton was pacing the room with a smirk on her smug face, glad to have captured harmless teenagers again. I wished that she was glad too soon, that someone, something, would get us out of this hopeless, endless turn of events.

Another turn of events took place, but this time in our favour. A woman came crashing into the room, with something in her hands that looked like a mini cannon. I wondered how these people had got here, but did not put much thought into it because there was no point.

A horde of people barged through the door, taking down Hanginton's people. Hanginton was looking real frustrated right about now, and I leered at her while I had the chance. As soon as we were out of the room, the room outside us disappeared, allowing Hanginton to escape. I wondered why the people who rescued us didn't kill her, and why we got dragged out of the room instead.

A woman with pink hair and blue eyes approached us. She had light brown skin, like *really* light, and… kind of had a lot of features like Hanginton.

"I'm Irene," she said. "I know this is gonna sound like a load of crap, but I'm Soundleek's sister."

There were collective unbelieving gasps. "Prove it." Sarthak demanded.

"Would the fact that the Marsians came to help me out of a home my sister trapped me in for about 10 years over a stupid feud count?"

That was a very Soundleek Hanginton thing to do. Trapping her own sister in a house for years? I could totally believe that.

"Doesn't sound sisterly," I mused.

"I agree. But please, you're just gonna have to believe me."

The four of us were still highly sceptical.

Irene saw Gertrude propped up in a corner. Her face lit up. "Is that Gertrude?"

"You know her?" Sarthak echoed our surprise.

"We worked together. Please wake her up."

After waking Gertrude up, we were told that Irene was indeed Soundleek's sister, and they knew each other. They talked for a little bit, maybe clearing things up.

It suddenly came to me that being rescued by Irene, who had been rescued by the Marsians, probably meant that we were going back to the Marsians.

I was not happy about it. It was the last place I wanted to be on in this universe. I did not want to have another crazy adventure and risk my life over it. I was over it, even though I thought about it every day of my life.

"I know what you are thinking," Irene said to us. "You don't want to risk your life. But you are safer where we're going. Hanginton is going to be on you if you stay on Earth."

"Why didn't you just kill her?" Pari said contemptibly.

"It wasn't possible," Irene replied, but something told me that was not the truth.

I guess we were staying. I wasn't happy about it, but we were surely staying. I was, deep down, feeling excited. I wondered how you could be unhappy and excited at the same time. Eh.

The Marsians were still in space, like some kind of intergalactic nomads. I wondered when they would find a home. But I guess it had only been a year, and I knew *nothing* about how to find a new planet where you must accommodate billions. I remembered they told us there were around a billion Marsian people, and looking at the size of the ship, I doubted that all of them were here. But they were really advanced in nanotech, so anything and any amount of people could be in that thing.

Being in space, however, reminded me of the *Baraak*. Even though it had been a year ago, the memory of the space monster still disgusted me. I don't really know why the *Baraak* was the one thing that I didn't like to think about. It made no sense, yet it lived rent-free in my head.

As soon as our ship docked into the humongous spacecraft of the Marsians, we were greeted by the General himself. The General and Glenda greeted each other, and the four of us warily eyed him. We didn't know what he had in store for us, because there was no way he was letting us stay here without any favours. I assumed that it was going to happen, and knowing the General's backstory, he would always seek something that could make his people more powerful and happy.

Gertrude had warned us. While he would mean no direct harm to us, he could potentially send us in situations that could harm us. But since we were in more danger on our own planet, I figured doing a few errands for the Marsians wouldn't be a problem.

And we had special uses. We were teenagers. We could fit in places not many people could, just because we had the face of children, even though in any guise we could have easily passed as adults. We were certainly the size of them. But with a few alterations, of course.

The General looked genuinely puzzled when he saw us giving him looks like he had just thrown someone off a cliff. As if reading my thoughts, he said, "Don't worry, I didn't throw anyone off a cliff."

All of us relaxed a little bit. A little bit. I wondered where all of this anxiety was coming from. We had tensed up like we were about to witness a natural disaster. This air of anxiety, when I had first met the General, had been nowhere to be found. I wondered why it was happening now.

"Yeah, we know," Pari said.

"So welcome to the temporary Marsian base," the General said.

"You got a billion people in here?" Yash said. From what I could remember from a year ago, the General didn't like being interrupted. Even the bot didn't like it. I saw Yash trying to keep a straight face and realized he had done it on purpose. I, however, allowed my smirk to show.

I liked to see people rage.

The General sighed in exasperation. "Yep. Nanotech," was all he said.

The General started to leave, and Gertrude followed him. They didn't tell us what we had to do though. But a moment later, we were approached by two people. We were told to follow them, and we did.

After walking for a bit, we arrived in what looked a hotel lobby. There were a lot of Marsians moving around. I realized this was their living quarters. It was like most hotel lobbies, even though the couches went on as far as the eye could see. This looked exactly like a hotel lobby, but a billion people lived here.

As I was feeling all small and philosophical, a Marsian guy came over to us and gave us a key. He told us to take an elevator to the floor were had to go to. As soon as we entered the lobby, I felt the same sensation I had felt when we had been in the Nanotech ship. It was a long time ago, but I remembered it. I realized that all of the lobbies were shrunk so that they could fit the people of Marsars in this big hunk o' something.

That sounded weird.

When we got to our rooms, I saw that it was like a normal hotel room, and I was confused. Why was a *Marsian* thingy so similar to earth?

Apparently, the person who led us here read our minds, and said, "The people who designed this ship found some things from your planet quite useful."

I realized that all of the Marsians knew about Earth, but none of us knew about Marsars. I guess when you were so ahead of one planet that you would obviously know more about everything around you. But it made me feel kinda nervous, because I was pretty sure the Marsians knew a lot about us as people as well. I felt like I was being monitored, and I didn't like it.

There was a bed, a TV, two tables beside the bed and a bathroom, and a window, which looked out into space and could - I noticed, alarmed - be opened. Yash actually opened it, and a screen appeared over the whole window, which allowed us to look better but prevented us from dying.

"Idiot," Pari said, which was one of the first things any of us had said in a long time.

Gertrude shouted something and made us all jump. I realized she was talking to someone outside the room.

She came in after that slightly alarming conversation and sat down on Sarthak's bed. There were 4 beds, one for each of us. I wondered what the Marsians did every day. Did they have jobs like we on earth did? Probably. I wondered what the Marsian currency was called.

"What do we do now?" Yash said.

"Absolutely nothing," Gertrude said. "Well, I gotta work a lot, but all of you are gonna be completely free for a *long* time."

"You mean until we can't go back to earth without getting killed?" Pari said.

"Yeah, that," Gertrude said.

We were free. I didn't really know what to do now, but I guess that we would figure something out sometime. For now, we just decided to hop into our beds. It was the most comfortable thing I had ever set foot on. That didn't sound right. I immediately sank into it and fell asleep.

The next morning, I was the last one who woke up. Sarthak was watching something on his phone eating chips, Yash was reading something as usual and Pari was in the bathroom.

"Morning," Yash said without looking up. I ran my hands through my hair and got up. For some reason, my feet were all wobbly when I got out of bed. I decided to sit back down and throw a pillow at Sarthak. The bag of chips left his hand, and fell down on the floor, along with most of the chips. He nonchalantly picked it back up, dirty chips and all, and started to eat them again. I almost gagged and decided to stop thinking about it.

Boys.

I noticed that there was another door near the bathroom, which turned out to be another bathroom. I quickly got in there to take a shower and decided to ignore another door right beside the door I had just opened. How was there even that much *space* on the wall for so many frickin doors? Nanotech was freaky.

Pari came out with me, and patted my wet hair. I slapped her with them for that.

"Ow," she said, and kicked me in the shin.

I decided to leave it at the kick on the shin before it escalated and one of us threw Sarthak's bag of chips at each other.

"We got literally nothing to do all day?" Sarthak sounded excited.

"Yeah," I said. "We could explore this place, but I kinda wanna spend the time here."

Before we could discuss how we were going to waste time the whole day, Gertrude entered the room. She took a look around the room and said, "I didn't expect a bunch of teenagers to keep a room so clean."

"You can thank Yash for that," Sarthak said. "If he sees anything out of place, he gets mad."

"That's not true," Yash said defensively, but there was no denying the truth.

"Anyways," Gertrude said. "We are gonna meet up with Selena and Tobias."

"Why?" Sarthak said sarcastically. "We kinda wanna spend the time in our rooms doing nothing."

"I can't tell if you are joking or serious," Yash said.

"I don't wanna meet them, idiot," Sarthak said. "Learn to take a hint." Sarthak snickered.

It was a poor joke, but Pari and I still burst into laughter, as all of us knew who he was talking about. Yash had had some… *unfortunate* experiences with a girl at school. Gertrude looked annoyed, but continued anyways.

"Come on, guys."

Sarthak raised his eyebrows and ran his hands through his hair. He didn't say anything, and neither of us did, because we knew that they had kind of put our lives on risk and used us. I still resented them for that.

"Give it a try," I said. "Maybe this time, they'll not tell us to risk our lives."

Gertrude sighed. "Look, I know you resent them for what happened, but…"

"Give them another chance? You got it," I said.

Gertrude put her hands in the air and said, "Ok I give up. It's up to you whether you wanna meet them right now. I'm gonna go eat something." She slowly walked out of the room and left the door open. All of us shouted at her to close it and she walked away. Yash got up to close it.

Pari broke the silence that had followed. "Do you want to meet them?"

"I don't mind," Yash replied. "We may as well, because we're kinda holed up in their ship and they're keeping us safe." It was the Marsians' ship, but we got the point.

Sarthak looked at him and scrunched up his nose. "Since when do *you* speak sensible things?"

Yash kicked him in the shin. Sarthak jumped around on one leg and then decided to keep his mouth shut.

"Ok then," I said. I called out to Gertrude. Gertrude came in with an expectant look. The creepy woman was standing right outside the door.

"Well?" she said and raised her eyebrows.

"We'll go," I said.

"Nice to know," Gertrude said.

We went out of the room into the lobby and then into the elevator. It was not a long ride up the elevator, but I could feel that it was going really fast. There was also the screen that indicated what floor we were on. After about ten seconds, we were on floor 221, the topmost floor of the whole hotel/living area of a billion people. It seemed to be the working space for people in space.

"It's the working place for people in space," I said. The four of them looked at me with what I thought were confused expressions, but it was disgust. "Do you not get it?" I repeated my joke.

"Oh, we get it," Yash said. "It's just one of the worst jokes you've ever made, and *any*one could have ever made."

I stuck my tongue at him. As if to add insult to injury, Gertrude said, "I'm a boomer, and even *my* humour is better than that."

Sarthak and Yash snorted like pigs. I mimicked them, but I couldn't do pigs quite well. That was not in my forte.

After some walking, we faced a big door. As soon as we knocked, an eye poked out of the door. I jumped back in surprise and realized it was a stupid camera. The camera buzzed and let us in. The door slid open with no sound whatsoever.

Selena and Tobias were sitting on chairs in the room. They greeted Gertrude. And nodded at us, looking kind of apologetic. I nodded back at them. Yash and Pari did that after me, but Sarthak didn't. He did have a history of holding grudges. He still had beef with a student at our school, and it has started about 5 years ago. I didn't exactly remember what had happened, but they had been good friends. The guy had tried to make it right but Sarthak was a stubborn guy.

He tried to smile. I could tell. But he just couldn't quite manage it. I almost snorted at the look on his face.

"Hey," Tobias said to break the ice.

"Hey," Yash said.

The awkwardness was so thick you could cut it.

"So why call us here?" Gertrude said.

"Well, we just wanted to meet the kids since out last encounter wasn't so… pleasant," Selena said sheepishly.

I instantly felt better about them. I realized that they thought they were sending us on a harmless mission. To be fair, we would have gotten out of there quite easily, but nobody hadn't considered that something this big could have happened right under the noses of the Namerians.

"So, what did you do about the Xinains?" Yash said out of the blue.

"We bombed the whole thing," Tobias said. "But they knew about it, so they had already evacuated."

It shocked me that they could take a decision to bomb a place where these were so many people, and so many casualties could have occurred. Maybe they didn't care about collateral? Banks wouldn't like them as much now.

This might have been my overthinking-teenage brain speaking to me, but I began thinking that this was basic human nature. Destroy everything you can't control. I almost laughed when I realized how true that was.

"Oh," Yash blurted out, and then there was silence again.

"Well, how are you guys?" Selena said, breaking it.

"For someone who's hiding from a psychopath, pretty good," I mused.

"Tell them why you sent them on a death mission," Gertrude said. Everyone looked at her furiously and Gertrude smirked. "You had to talk about it *some*time, right?"

"Yeah, I hoped that sometime would be never," Sarthak said.

"So did we," Tobais said. For some reason, we found it funny and laughed at that.

"We want to show you something," Selena said.

"What is it?" Gertrude asked her.

"Come with us." She got up from her seat and went to a corner in the room, where she pressed something and doors opened. There was a secret elevator in the room. I wasn't even surprised.

"What does this lead to?" Gertrude said.

"Underground," I said.

Gertrude looked at me with a disgusted expression. I smirked back at her.

All of us got into the elevator. The elevator was pretty big. About 15 people could have fit in there. The doors closed with almost no sound, and we started to *ascend*.

"Wasn't that the top floor?" Yash said.

"Yes," Tobias said and smirked. He provided no further explanation. I didn't like people who liked drama, but I decided to make an exception for Tobias, because I really liked him. I didn't like Selena that much because she gave me vibes of an evil maniac. I decided to shake it off for then.

We were in the elevator for about a minute. The elevator stopped, and the doors opened to a hot and stuffy room. We immediately started sweating.

We got out of the door, and there was a woman wearing a suit that covered her full body. I wondered why it was, and I got closer to the door, curious. I jumped back with a yelp. The room inside was definitely very hot, and the suits must be to protect ourselves from the intense heat.

The person didn't even notice us until we were close. She was on a phone.

"Get off the phone, man," Tobias groaned. "Somebody's gonna burn due to that damn phone."

"Never say *man* again, please, Tobias," she said. "Why do you have kids with you? You got a plan to burn them?"

"She doesn't mean it," Tobias told us.

"No way!" Sarthak intoned.

The woman handed out clasps. "Put these on the top of your head, and press the button."

We did as we were told, and a suit enclosed us. We had an opening near the eyes, The woman pressed a button, a door opened and we went in. As the door was closing, I saw her go back to her phone and I smirked at her. She returned it.

I could practically see the heat in the room. But there seemed to be a built in AC in our suit, and my body cooled down as soon as the heat in our surroundings increased.

There were many people in the room. They were very short people. It reminded me of fairies.

"Are these-?" Pari said.

"Fairies? Yes," Selena said. She smirked as she saw the look of surprise on our faces.

"Why is the room this hot?" Gertrude asked.

"Because of the magic they perform," Tobias said. "Whenever magic is performed on something that has a lot of energy, like ship engines, or even blasters, immense heat is produced. If you were in this room without your suits, you'd be boiled alive in a few minutes."

I waited for a laugh but none came.

"Wait, you're serious?" Pari said. Apparently, everyone felt like that last statement should have been a joke.

"Yes," Tobias said.

"So why bring *us* here?" Sarthak said.

"No reason. We just wanted to show you something we had been working on."

"Why *us*?" Sarthak said again.

"Because we wanted to brag, okay!" Tobias said. Everybody burst laughing at that, except, I noticed, Selena. I wondered if she thought the joke was unfunny. Tobias looked pretty happy at everybody laughing at his statement.

They led us towards the centre of the room. The fairies paid us no attention. All of them were working on something in the humongous room. There were weapons, bracelets, and so many other things. In the middle of the room, on a table, there was a giant piece of machinery, about 20 feet in width and *very* tall. I had to arch my neck up to see its end.

"Is this a weapon?" I asked Tobias.

"We can't tell you what it is, but it's not a weapon," he replied.

I just couldn't take his word for it – and losing count of how many times I had – and decided to let it go. The machine was magnificent. It was a mixture of dark blue and grey, and had grooves all over its body. But other than that, there was nothing outside the thing.

We headed out of the room and went to the elevator. As soon as we got out of the elevator, someone burst into the room. He looked worried.

He looked worried. "Nameri is being attacked." Tobias and Selena's expressions drastically changed.

"Say what now?" Tobias said.

"I stand by what I said, sir," the man said. "They want you in the Whizari headquarters right now."

Tobias and Selena said to Gertrude, "Come with us. We may need you."

Gertrude didn't agree. "No. I'm staying here with the kids." I was actually touched, but I knew she wanted to go.

"Go," I told her.

"But… ok." She sighed. "I'll go. Don't burst this ship open the moment I go, ok?"

"Yeah, we'll try," I grinned at her. She didn't return it. Gertrude went out of the room.

As soon as she was out of the room, a portal opened in the room and 2 people came out of it. They had body suits on and what looked like tasers in their hands. As soon as I figured out what was happening, I was unconscious.

CHAPTER 7

Abduction

When I woke up, my head was spinning. I tried to get up but I was tied to my seat. The four of us were in a small room, and all of us woke up at around the same time, in the span of a few seconds. I was still feeling dizzy for a few minutes after. I was losing track of how many minutes had passed. I noticed that there was no sound from the room we were in. We could literally be anywhere.

"Hi," was all I was able to get out before I collapsed and fell asleep.

I woke up with starts and fits. Whenever I woke up, I could see my friends collapsed in their chairs. For some reason, it made me want to *not* get up.

It was like how drugged sleeps were described. Slipping into and out of oblivion, feeling that empty tug in your stomach. I couldn't keep track of time, so I just decided to give up.

But it kept happening. I woke up and slept. It was a never-ending cycle. It was getting really annoying. I wanted to get up and kick someone. I was pretty sure I did kick someone when I was in my stupor, but it didn't faze anybody. I couldn't even feel anything anywhere on my body. It was the best feeling in the world and yet there was that drugged-sleep-type sleep.

Towards the end of our stupor, I remembered seeing someone walk in our room and turn the lights off. I thought they did, anyway.

I woke up from my stupor after they went out of the room. There was now a slight humming voice coming from outside the room, which made me almost certain we were floating in space, because all of these spaceships made the same sort of sound.

"What the-" Pari said a questionable word. "Where are we?"

"Why would we know?" I gave her.

She made a face at me. "Rhetorical question, stupid."

"Ah," I felt stupid.

"Dude, what is our luck?" Sarthak groaned.

"Bad?" Yash groaned back at him.

"Thanks, Sherlock." He groaned back.

I put my head in my hands. My head hurt from all that was happening, and the fact that we had been kidnapped again for the umpteenth time. I wasn't even fazed now. But judging by our surroundings and the hum of what seemed to be a ship, we were probably floating around in space. I wanted to slap my six-year-old self that had wanted to become an astronaut.

But I was hopeful. We would find a way.

"My head hurts," somebody said.

"Same," somebody agreed.

There was some quiet, and then someone opened the door and came in. Their face was completely covered because they wore a white suit, covering the whole body except for slits so that they could see.

We were handed microphone-like thingys. I wondered what we were supposed to do with them. The person came over and put it wherever it was supposed to be.

The person – a man, I assumed due to his voice – spoke, "Follow me. Do one thing I tell you not to and you'll be dead before you can say sorry."

The four of us nodded in unison. I gulped.

All of my thoughts hit me like a train. Why were we kidnapped. What did they want with *us*? Of all the people on the Marsians' ship, why were *we* important? I finally knew what anxiety was. As my mind bombarded me with questions, we entered a long passage. There were no doors in the walls. It made me wonder why there was such a long, narrow passage that existed for no apparent reason.

We finally made it to the end of the passage. My experience in space and space-related stuff was *highly* filled with long passages. It kind of made me realize how big these things were.

We got to the door, and the man held each of our backs at gunpoint as we were led in. I was the last one to go in. There room seemed to be small, but I could see a screen in front of us. That screen dropped like a curtain and we were greeted with the sight of the woman with black hair in a T-shirt and jeans.

My heart constricted in fear. I actually felt faint. I wondered where that deep set fear of the woman came from. All she did was try to kill us.

I almost laughed out loud at those words. *Just try to kill us.* it amused me how easily I could say these words and *mean* them.

The woman was just standing and smiling at us. Strangely, she didn't seem as intimidating and scary as the last time we saw her. But she also wasn't glowing purple. Purple was a terrifying colour. She looked like a normal person right now, but I expected her to morph into a witch any moment.

I couldn't stomach the fact that this was the woman who almost killed us, since she was also kind of short. She was shorter than me.

"I know you're wondering why you are here," she started. "But let me introduce myself first. I'm Sayon." It sounded exactly like say-on. Weird name.

"I'm the general of the army of the council of Xin. It is a coalition of all the countries present in Xin, and deals with aliens and outer space stuff." She sat down on a chair. "I also happen to know a little bit of magic, as you already might know." She smirked at us. I wanted to slap her and strangely laugh at the same time. If she hadn't tried to kill us before, I would have liked her. She seemed... *human.*

"I know you fear me," she said. "And you should, because I can kill you with a snap of my finger. That was cringe."

"Glad you realize," I blurted out, immediately regretting it.

She shot me a look that reminded me of my mom when she was angry, but ignored me. "We have brought you here because last time you saw me, you unknowingly took something valuable with you."

We looked at each other in confusion. What was she talking about?

"What you took was magic, some that we had been searching for about a decade."

Her words hit me like a brick. We stole… *magic?* I was pretty sure my face was as dumbstruck as the faces of my friends was.

"What do you mean, *took* some magic?" Yash asked.

"We found residues of the said magic in your DNA after you left the compound. What the magic does, however, I'll obviously not tell you. And I still have no clue how it got into you, but I guess life has its ups and downs, huh?

"All I need you to know is that we will go to any length to extract the pieces of magic from you, even if it requires taking it out from your corpse."

She spoke this matter-of-factly. She didn't see how hard my heartbeat in that moment. To know that my life was not in my own hands was terrifying, more than anything I had ever known. My legs were quaking in their boots. First time I had ever used the phrase unironically.

Just when we had thought this was all behind us, it had come back at us like a boomerang.

"What do we need to do?" I sounded defiant, but I think she knew that I was faking. The woman smiled. My friends looked at me like I was crazy.

She sounded happy. "Good, so you do understand."

She shot a fierce look at my friends. "Do you?"

"Yes," they croaked.

She laughed. "Good. Now we'll leave you to it."

Why did she scare the crap out of us? Right now, she was the most unremarkable witch I had ever seen, but my legs hadn't stopped shaking.

She pressed a button on the desk and four bunk beds popped out. She and the man who brought us in and went out of the room. The desk folded in on itself and disappeared into the ground.

Sarthak breathed in relief as soon as she went out of the room. "At least we're alive." We heard a click and I realized that the room had been locked. As if we could go anywhere.

"Yeah," Yash said.

Nobody said anything for a moment. Then I said, "Why the HELL do we have magic?"

"I know, right," Yash agreed with me. We looked at him, cringing.

"Who says that out loud?" Pari sounded disgusted.

"Move on."

"What do we do now?" I felt helpless.

"Comply." I kept forgetting he had really good vocabulary. But the word was scary, as if we were slaves.

"So, we're like servants?" Sarthak sounded defeated.

"Pretty much," Pari sighed. "But if we make a mistake, we die. All we can hope is to live right now, and hope for rescue. But I doubt that's happening."

That cheerful statement left us silent for some time.

"When do you think we inherited this magic?" Yash finally spoke up.

"*Stole*," Sarthak said aggressively, like he was telling somebody to shut up. "And I think it was when we were in the compound, you know, like she *just told us*."

Yash frowned. "You know what I mean."

"I know, it's fun making fun of you."

I lay down on the bed and closed my eyes. I was out like a light in a moment. I don't even know how I managed to fall asleep. I didn't even realize I was tired.

When I woke up, it was like I was in a stupor again. It felt disconcerting. I supposed it must have been the aftereffects of whatever we had been given. As I tried to stand up, my legs gave away and I fell back on the bed. But I couldn't sleep now, for some reason.

I felt disconnected from the world. I couldn't understand anything as of now. How we were going to get the magic out of us, and if we could somehow use it.

I suddenly sat up. We could *use* that magic. But with dismay I realized Sayon and the Xinains couldn't be that dumb. They had to have taken all the variables in and then capture us.

I decided to ask her the next day. I laid back down and took my phone out, surprisingly, this place had Wi-Fi, one that I could connect my phone to. I wondered how, but didn't care that much.

I watched some videos and before I knew, my friends woke up. Pari woke up and sat up on her bed. She looked at me like I was an insane person.

"Why are you looking at me like that?" I asked her.

"You look like you've seen someone die," she told me gently, and came down to sit beside me. I put my hands in my head and silently shook forwards and backwards.

"Since when are you the mom?" I laughed.

Pari smirked. "You do remember I'm a year older than you."

"Ok, boomer."

Sarthak moved on his bed, and said something inappropriate, words that heavily hinted we shut up.

"What are you talking about?" he said, getting up, feigning interest. He saw my face and he actually gained interest. "You good?" He had that awkward look of not knowing what to do that people often had in these situations.

"Yeah," I lied to him.

"Good," he replied, looking at his phone. Pari and I looked up at him, flabbergasted that he thought I was serious. "By the way, did you know there was Wi-Fi?" Sarthak looked up from his phone.

"Yeah," I said again. "I was on my phone for the past hour."

He grinned. "I'm pretty sure our parents will be 'It's the phone's fault' if they see you like this." I slapped his arm but giggled along with them.

Yash woke up too, "due to all the ruckus", which wasn't honestly much, but it sounded funny when he called it a 'ruckus'.

I rubbed my eyes and sighed. Whatever awaited us after this was not pleasant. I was pretty sure that the Xinains would kill us if it meant getting the magic they wanted. All we could do, for now, was hope.

I had to tell this to myself every moment.

Hope.

CHAPTER 8

Magic DNA

We were called into Sayon's office after we were ready. It was strange how we always found time to shower and stuff before these bizarre adventures. Our room was like a normal room on earth, but I noticed Sayon's wasn't. The bed was different, shaped for adjusting the Xinains' long bodies. They were also taller than the average human.

"Welcome." Sayon was wearing what looked like armour to me, which was strange because we were just in an office. "We'll analyse you today."

"You'll what?" Yash shared the words with my inner monologue.

"Analyse. We're going to see what percentage of the magic is in your DNA now."

"How is it in our DNA?" Pari, the biology nerd, asked Sayon.

"It just is."

Pari looked befuddled. "So… how did they get there? Editing?"

"Edit what?" Yash looked up from his phone.

"Our genes, genius," Sarthak said, slapping his arm.

"For editing, we would have to do it ourselves," Sayon said. She seemed a bit impressed we knew what gene editing was. What did she think humans were? Maggots? It was hilarious to me. It was the cliché 'aliens think humans are inferior'. "It was magic. That's all you need to know for now."

"What do you mean, for now?"

"That's what I said."

Sarthak shrugged. His face was the embodiment of *'Okay, I guess'.*

"So, what are we going to do?" Yash asked her.

Sayon slammed her desk. "Alright, one more question, and I *will* throw you out of this spaceship."

"Somebody's got anger issues…" I mocked her in a sing-song voice. I knew she couldn't afford to kill any of us, and for some reason I decided to call her bluff.

She breathed so loudly I practically saw smoke coming out of her mouth. It was amusing.

Her hand gripped her table really hard. "I really, really wanna kill you."

"Same," Pari said.

Sayon raised her eyebrows and took a deep breath. "You kids are annoying. Follow me."

She started to walk out of the room and we followed her. For someone who had almost killed us when we had first seen her, she seemed like a pretty chill person. I wondered if her almost killing us was just for scaring us. but that didn't seem like her. She seemed to make tactical decisions all along the way. Using scare factors didn't seem like it was exactly how she would go along, but no one knew how she worked.

We started towards what was probably a lift. The topic of how alien life was similar to the humans had always interested me, and as of right now, it was pretty similar to us.

The lift opened up and Sayon pressed a switch. The buttons seemed to be numbers in another language. We reached the floor in about 2 seconds. The door opened into a small room. There was only space for about ten people in there, and in the centre of the room were 5 glass cylinders with door. This was probably where the analysing was gonna happen. There was a metal bar outside the glass cylinders. They were really, *really* similar to those airport X-Ray machines.

"Get in 'em," Sayon told us. "It won't take long, at least in real time."

"What?"

"You'll be showed a simulation in there. It will help while you're being analysed."

"Why'll it help?" I asked her.

"When you're in our simulation, you have no thoughts. You just exist, just another hunk of flesh in this universe. It just helps us."

That sounded terrifying yet tempting to me. Having no thoughts for some time would be nice.

"Alright then," Sayon said. "Get in."

We did and the doors opened and closed automatically. Metal arms grabbed my arm and ankles. The metal brace around the container went down, shooting out some rays, and I was in the simulation.

My simulation world was simple. It had a few trees, but at the horizon, I could see what seemed like blurred images. It was calm here, and this whole landscape seemed to go around the middle like a concentric circle, like a boundary. I started to walk towards the centre.

"It's so calm," I said to myself.

As the centre approached, the landscape got more ragged. As the centre got closer, I saw that it on was fire.

"Why is it fire?" I spoke. "I can't have thoughts so I'm speaking it aloud."

I cringed at that, and decided to shut up. "I should shut up."

My nostrils flared in annoyance. I never thought complete sentences, but my simulation-self had to use correct grammar.

I arrived at something like a border of my simulation. There was a blue, sizzling force-field around the area ravaging with fire.

"What-" was all I could say before I was yanked out of the simulation.

The world hit me like a brick as soon as my eye opened. It was so messy, so chaotic in my brain. I loved it in the simulation. I had been there for hours with no thoughts. It was pleasant.

I stumbled out of the container and grabbed Sarthak's arm for support. My legs felt weak.

"How long were we in there?" I asked Sayon.

"About two minutes," she said. "We found where the magic was nested pretty quickly."

"And?" Yash sounded excited. I guess having magic in yourself does induce excitement. I just couldn't find that excitement.

"You whole body. You have a *big* chunk of magic inside you. You can even use it if you learn." She referred to magic as if it was some kind of physical substance.

"What?"

"Yeah. But if you do, it'll kill you in the fraction of a second. Humans are fragile."

"What do we have to do to return home?" Pari cut her off.

"It's a long process. You see, for getting the magic out of someone, there is a ritual. That ritual can be done on Xin. We can get near the site of ritual, but the magic radiating out of that place disables any technology within a 50-kilometre radius. So, we'll have to get there by foot and some magical weapons. Even Technomagic is useless there. The fact that it's on an unsurmountable mountain makes it much worse."

There was pin-drop silence in the room. We would have to go through hell to get that magic out of us. We may even die. But for some reason, I wasn't afraid.

I *wanted* to do it.

I wanted the thrill of an adventure again. I wasn't afraid for my life. I wanted to be in danger again. Weird how that worked.

"When do we leave?" I looked at Sayon, apparently my friends seemed to agree with me. It seemed like all of us were ready and eager to go on a goddamn suicide mission again. I wondered why my crazy, teen brain wanted that. It wasn't like we had a choice anyway.

"In a week of earth days," Sayon said. "So, a week for us as well."

That statement made zero sense.

I wondered how many hours their day was, but decided to let it be. A week was a long time to be free before impending doom. I wasn't excited about this. I wondered if we could explore the ship. Before I could say that out loud, Sayon started speaking.

"You won't be allowed outside a designated area, and if you try to disobey us, you're gonna be floating in space."

On that cheerful note, we were dismissed from the lab. A woman came to escort us to our 'designated area'. It was pretty large, made for maybe housing an important family? I wondered why *we* were given a staying place here. I guess we were important to the Xinains. I wondered if they would actually kill us if we disobeyed them. For some reason, I was really tempted to try out something stupid. I pinched myself. I didn't need thoughts like that if I didn't wanna go insane.

"I don't know how, but we always end up waiting for a few days before action commences," Yash mused. "Like we're bored one second and we're jumping off a building into a plane next."

"When'd that happen?" I asked him.

"When we got into Glenda's plane. Sarthak broke his arm, remember?"

"Thanks for reminding me," Sarthak winced and slapped Yash on his head.

"But I never got to know how it broke," I said, smirking.

"It was stupid," Sarthak muttered.

Pari snorted. "The idiot's finger got stuck in a broken pillar."

Yash and I burst out laughing. Sarthak smiled, kind of embarrassed.

There was sudden silence after all of us were done laughing. I realized the four of us hadn't had a moment where we had *really* laughed since so long. This 'adventure' was sucking out our joys of being in our teenage. I almost snorted out loud when that thought came to me, and how much it sounded like it came out of a cheesy movie, which it probably did.

The week passed without much happening. The four of us were just loafing around, waiting for the day where we could get out of our prison/nice room. None of us were stupid enough to risk it for the biscuit, even though I had several urges to walk out and just cause trouble. I knew I would get thrown out into space, but haven't most of us had that urge, the urge to see what was going to happen? To jump off a building, jump in front of a car? Or I was just insane.

Our room was simple, with 4 beds, 2 bathrooms, a TV and for some reason a PS4 with no controllers that none of us had touched. We had Wi-Fi, and our phones. 4 teenagers with phones and Wi-Fi didn't get bored. If they did, there was something wrong with them. Fortunately, none of us were insane and used our phones like sane people would.

One random night started thinking how much I had changed these last 2 years. Sarthak and Yash were pretty much towering over me and Pari now. All of us were so much more mature. I couldn't remember the last time I just had *fun* though. Before all this, after those two weeks, I was miserable because I had nothing to do. I was cooped up in my home all day, and wasn't having any interest in anything in this mortal world. My mind had kept going back to this thrill of adventure. I wondered if I would ever be able to stay put after this.

But that was a question for later.

The seven days were over in what seemed a heartbeat. A shuttle that looked like an egg was prepared for us. It was about the size of a small house, and grey. I had a weird urge to kick the shuttle to see if it would collapse like an egg did. I decided to pass off that urge because I didn't wanna get yeeted into space.

The inside of the shuttle was, for some reason, all dark blue. It was like LED strips were the main lighting area of the ship.

"Why blue?" Yash said. I expected some weird Xinain-related reason, because that was what everything had been till now.

"I like it," Sayon said. I almost giggled.

Inside the ship, it was just the four of us, Sayon and a woman who was sleeping on her stomach on what seemed to be a couch, but it was a weird shape. It stooped down to half its height randomly in the middle, and went back up like a very steep parabola. There was nothing in the middle, just the woman's stomach above the gap. I wondered what the hell was that and why it existed.

Sayon went to the woman and slammed her back. She let out a startled gasp and sat up straight. She said questionable words to Sayon when she saw her.

"Who are these clowns?" she said, looking at us. I had a weird feeling this woman wasn't from Xin. From what I had seen, Xinains were usually tall and lanky, Sayon being the exception. This woman was neither.

"This is Anita," Sayon said to us. "She's going to be the lead for this mission." Anita realised who we were at that point. I was pretty sure Anita wasn't something a Xinain would be named.

I was pretty sure that meant Sayon wasn't coming with us.

"Get up, you slouch," Sayon said, casting a disgruntled look at Anita. Anita made a face at her and got up. They had the chemistry of very good friends. Anita looked at us and smiled.

"Ah, they're the poor magic kids you abducted," she intoned.

"Well, if we hadn't abducted them, they would have been dead within like 2 years anyways," Sayon said nonchalantly. I was pretty sure she was speaking in a monotone and kind of like a teacher's voice to piss us off.

"We *what*?" Sarthak shouted, followed by similar exclamations by the rest of us.

"Your body is too weak for that kind of magic. Your organs would have failed little by little until you would just be a vegetable."

"Thanks for the description," Yash sounded disgusted. I was suddenly grateful to my abductor, even though she couldn't have cared less if we did not have her magic and died.

"So how long will we take to get there?" Pari asked.

"About 5 minutes," Anita told us. "As Sayon may have told you, technology cannot be used to get there. It is going to be one long journey, and *cold*. The path to the cave is gonna be covered with snow *completely*."

"Again, thank you for the description," I said dryly. I was not thrilled now. I hated the winters. But I could wear awesome hoodies. I cringed at myself. That was the most teenager thought that had ever come to my mind, but somehow, I didn't mind. I decided to leave my messed-up brain alone.

Anita started to go to what I assumed was the front of our egg.

"Please take your seats," a voice from a speaker above us made me jump.

Seats popped out of the ground. All of us sat on it, while Sayon left the ship. The moment the doors of the Egg closed, there was a humming sound and we were off.

"If you leave your seats right now, you will experience some *very* heavy turbulence," Anita said on what I assumed was the intercom. I sat back in my seat and decided to think about what we were about to do. This could very easily get us all killed, but for some reason my brain couldn't comprehend, I was excited. What was wrong with me?

Before I knew it, we were there. I didn't know what *there* was, because nobody had told us. The egg suddenly became fully transparent. I couldn't see a thing around us because of all the snow. I was pretty sure if we went out right now, we would be as frozen as an icicle. An exaggeration, but that is what I felt. There was a raging blizzard outside the Egg, and ice as white as… it was the *whitest* thing I had ever seen. I wasn't sure if it was a word.

Before I knew it, I saw the Egg getting engulfed by snow from the blizzard. I couldn't deny that what I had been seeing of the landscape before had been breathtakingly beautiful.

"Make this thing non-transparent!" Yash panicked.

"Why?" Anita was genuinely confused. "I love this. Just solace."

"Solace, my foot. My eyes hurt."

"Same," the three of us said at the same time and snickered.

Anita sighed and the ship turned back to its original state. All of this technology was making me awe and make my head hurt at the same time.

"When are we going out?" Sarthak asked Anita.

"When this goddamn blizzard fades," she said. "There'll be a lot of snow still, and it will be *cold*, but we can go out then."

Why couldn't this ritual thing just be somewhere where there was good weather? What was it with important things and bad weather? I hadn't seen it happen to us, but it always happened in movies or books. Every important thing was either somewhere extremely hot or extremely cold. I guess it was to protect the important stuff, but why did it have to be real?

"So how long?" Yash said.

"Hell, if I knew," Anita said. "It's gonna be at least 12 hours, so make yourselves cosy, and take these clothes. They're the magic powered thingies supposed to protect us."

She snapped her finger and a cupboard popped out of the ground. She told us to take the clothes from in there. They were nothing special, they were black, and I assumed they would adjust themselves to our size. I was totally gonna take one of these back home, and freak some people out. If I ever got home.

See, that's why I didn't like myself. Now I was sad.

There were only t-shirts in the cupboard. I assumed there would be another cupboard and put it on. It engulfed me completely, and it was so soft. I ran my hand over the fabric.

My friends had their t-shirts over them too. I wondered why they would use nanotech for frickin clothes.

"Tomorrow, we go," Anita said with affirmation.

Tomorrow came and I wasn't glad. For some reason, all my excitement of yesterday had faded. It was most probably due to being cooped up inside a transparent egg. But as time went on and on, I started dreading the cold, the fact that we may die started to become obvious to me.

"We leave now," Anita told us over the intercom. I hadn't taken off the clothes Anita had given us.

I took in a deep breath, and we walked out of our room. Anita gave us masks.

"These are oxygen masks, and they're gonna protect your faces from the cold. Take these off and you're dead."

Each of us were given a backpack. Inside the backpack were things like food, extra clothes, water that was connected through a tube through our mask. There were enough resources to last us for a year. Or so Anita said. I hadn't gone through the bag properly, but I was convinced that there were enough things to help us survive.

We had two guns that were about the size of a 500 ml bottle. They glowed whenever they were in our hands, but they had a button to turn it off. What were with these guns and glowing? It sure as hell did not look good. If they thought it looked good, they needed help. The gun was like an actual rifle, with the barrel, the trigger and all the other attachments. I was pretty sure Sarthak and Yash would know what the hell they were called. Or what their Call of Duty equivalents would be.

As sayon had told us, the gun worked on pure magic. I wondered if the rifles humans used had electricity in them. Most probably, the answer to that question was no. I wondered why we weren't using guns from Earth.

"If magic isn't allowed, why aren't we using guns from Earth?" I asked Anita.

"Because guns from our planet will kill anything its bullets touch on this planet. We don't like that."

"You sound like my mom," I said.

"Why?"

"It's too 'violent,'" I said with hand quotes.

Anita snickered. "That sounds familiar." Her face suddenly got sad.

"What happened?"

"I miss my mom. I miss my family." she gripped the gun she was holding tightly. "They were killed by the damn Hanginton's people 13 years ago. All because they opposed them."

My parents were also killed by the Hangintons around that time. I wondered what was happening then. Soundleek had even trapped her sister. The woman could go any bonds to get what she wanted.

Well, so could I.

"If you don't mind me asking, how old are you?"

"I'm 26," she said. Then she was also about my age when she got to know about it.

"What's your story?" Anita asked me.

"Me? Well, we got kidnapped on a vacation, met a rich farmer, she got kidnapped, we rescued her, then we got kidnapped again, then we escaped, stopped Soundleek from killing a lot of people on earth. That was after we stopped her from making everybody deaf on our planet so she could their eardrums or something," I said, and took a breath. "I'm sorry, I'm rambling."

"No, no, go on," Anita said. "Also, there's a *lot* of kidnapping going on."

I laughed. "I guess. We got home after that, and here we are a year later, kidnapped again."

Anita raised her eyebrows. "That's a lot happening in a small amount of time. How're you holding up?"

"Honestly, it's bad. I don't know what anything is anymore."

Anita kept a hand on my shoulder and squeezed. "It's gonna be alright."

I could only hope. It warmed my heart that Anita wasn't like these monsters.

CHAPTER 9

Blizzards. And Birds…?

Anita made sure we had everything before opening the doors of the Egg. It was pretty bad outside our ship, and I had no want of going outside this comfortable elliptical sphere. That was a shape that did not exist. I was pretty sure we were in an ellipsoid. Anita gave us microphones and headphones, and our masks. We connected that to the water in our bags.

I went over to Pari while Anita checked stuff. "Are you excited? I don't know what's wrong with me, but I am."

Pari smiled. "Don't worry, I am too."

"You haven't been talking much all this time," I said to her. "You've changed so much the last two years." She looked sheepish at those words. "Talk to me, you big-" My words were lost as Anita opened the doors of the Egg and a door closed behind us. The sound was muffled for me, but oh it was *loud*. And the cold. My whole body was shivering in a second as soon as the atmosphere around me changed.

Anita had told us that the microphones could control who we wanted to talk to. I wondered how the hell they knew what we were thinking, but that just made me sound like some old, complaining idiot. *Our phones can hear our conversations.* I hated those people.

We just had to use the mics until we got to the caves, where it would be easy to talk. I wondered what the temperature was, according to Earth people. It had to be something like -50 Celsius. I had never felt it, but this is what I imagined it to be.

"What is the temperature here?" Sarthak said over the mic. It was probably to everybody.

"It is about -130 degree Celsius," Anita said.

"It *what*?" Yash said. "And how are we not feeling cold at all?"

I looked at Yash sceptically, wondering why he didn't feel the cold, and the door of the Egg behind us closed. I couldn't see a frickin path in all of the snow, but I guess Anita had some sort of compass.

"You can stop using the mic if you want to," Anita said, not over the headset. "It's surprisingly not very windy."

"How do we turn it off?" Sarthak said.

"Just… uh, think that you don't wanna use it."

I did that and heard a beep of it turning off. Again, I wondered how.

I walked over to Pari, who was the last in the group. We were not going up or down, just walking in a load of snow at the same elevation.

"How are you?" I asked her.

"I'm good, genius," she said, and gripped my hand.

I raised my eyebrows. "You can't see my raising my eyebrows, but I know you. You like to talk."

She let out a sigh. "I guess you're right. I'm horrible. It was kinda hard at home, and now we are most probably going on a suicide mission. I don't really know what to feel anymore."

I felt that. "It'll get better. They say it does anyway."

She laughed at that. "We can only hope."

I almost laughed, because hope was one of the only things we had right about now.

"Yep," I said, and pulled her ahead, the others were at what seemed like the beginning of a mountain.

"This conversation was the most I've ever cringed," Pari said.

I giggled. "Same."

Pari and I got there and I looked up at the vastness of the big hunk o' rock above us. It was breathtakingly beautiful, and at the same time terrifying. It reminded me how un-impactful I was to the world. I guess the magic in me was important, but right now, it was nothing to me. It was just something for Sayon to farm out of us.

Sarthak compared the mountain to the size of something else and the four of us burst out laughing. Anita didn't look amused.

She frowned. "Your sense of humour needs some help.".

"I don't think it's *ours* that needs help," Sarthak said.

"Do you want me to throw you off this mountain?" she asked Sarthak, and she seemed serious.

"You can try."

"God, these teenagers."

"I know, we all need help."

Anita raised her hands in surrender and said, "We need to scale that big thing. For now, we can rest, because doing that is going to take at least 6 hours, and it's going to get pretty dark pretty fast, and even colder."

"By the way, we don't have a deadline of some sort, do we?" Yash said.

"No, I hope not," Anita said.

"What do you mean?"

"I don't know," Anita said. "But if some high-ranking magic warlock gets angry at someone, we may have a problem."

"What are you even talking about?" I asked her, confused.

"The fairies have a whole order of ranks of warlocks," she answered. "I don't want to explain farther because I have crossed my limit."

"Of what?"

"Of dealing with clueless kids."

At the word kids, the four of us cast accusing glances at her. She snickered. "Help me set up our tents."

We went over to her, and found a comparatively flat surface in all of the snow. I think we had been here for about 2 hours, and in those 2 hours I had realized that I could, in fact, hate something I had loved all my life. We had gone to mountainous parts of India so many times, I would almost always see white blankets of white snow every year. But something about this snow felt… different. It seemed *whiter*. I wondered if that was even possible.

The wind was whispering, and Anita was saying that it would just keep getting worse. She said if we didn't set our tents up faster, we would be blown away like paper in a leaf blower. That was a very strange description, but she said it with a hint of sadness, and I think all of us decided to leave it at that. I wondered what the story was behind that, and why such a weird phrase reminded her of it.

We got the tent out, and it expanded. It left behind a few sparks of red and yellow, and I decided that was magic. I really hoped it wasn't electrostatic because if it was, we were in for some major shocks.

The tent was the size of an apartment, and it gave me the tent from *Goblet of fire* vibes. I was about to say '*I love magic*' out loud but one of the hooks the tent was on violently detached itself.

"What?" Anita said. 'This shouldn't be possible-"

She yelled out loud as a tentacle type thing grabbed her arm. It pulled her to the ground. She whipped a knife out and cut the tentacle. She brushed the blood, which was purple, off of her.

"We're not on top of a rock," she said.

Given our luck, I wasn't even surprised.

"I don't know what the hell this is," she told us, and tapped the tent somewhere and it went back to its original size. "Keep your guns out. We can encounter things like these again."

For some reason, I wasn't scared at all. I was kind of excited to fight what was technically a space monster.

All of us had our guns out, and Anita was just with her knife. The blade looked sharp and was stained purple with the blood of the creature that was below us right now. The tentacle she had cut off was throbbing beside us. Thankfully, there was no space to fall off of around us, so in case the creature below us decided to awaken, we would be thrown into snow and not into an abyss. We had ziplines and stuff, but I doubted any of us could manage to throw out a hook and save ourselves. This was no Bahubali movie.

There was an ear-splitting roar below us and Anita yelled, "Get off!", and we just made it off as the rock below us rose into a five-metre tall... rock? From what I could see, it had the texture of a rock, with eyes and a surprisingly small mouth. I mean, it was still big, but a creature that big should most probably have a bigger mouth. From what I could see, its tentacles hadn't made an appearance as of now.

Just as that thought came to my mind, several tentacles emerged out the ground. They came out of rock, injuring themselves in the process. The white tentacles, stained now with purple, and the rock-monster with googly eyes made a surprisingly funny and terrifying image at the same time. Without thinking, I shot my gun at its eye. It let out another ear-splitting shriek and what I assumed was a fart because *God* the smell was bad.

"Shoot its eyes!" Anita shouted over the groans of the monster. "Just follow me, we can't kill it!"

As told, we started shooting. The bullets hit hits eyes repeatedly and its tentacles came after us. Anita whipped out her knife and yelled. She charged at the monster without telling us to stop shooting. Thank God our stray shots didn't hit her.

She ran *towards* the tentacles and cut one off like it was nothing. 3 more shot themselves in her direction, and she finessed them, cutting one off in the process. While she was fighting them, others came after us.

I whipped out my knife, because shooting it was doing nothing to them. 2 of them came at us speedily, and slapped us into the snow like we were flies.

"Someone come fight one of these things with me, the other two go fight the other!" I yelled, getting up.

Sarthak ran to me while Pari ran to Yash. His knife was out, and we steadied our feet.

"You ready?" I asked him.

He puffed his chest up and mockingly said, "My whole life has been for this moment."

One tentacle zapped its way to us and we sluggishly dodged it. The next time it came, the both of us grabbed it.

"You hold, I'll cut it off!" I told Sarthak. Cutting it off some distance would do the job for now, but we needed to get away from the monster to stop it from coming at us again.

He nodded and grunted when I left the tentacle. I decided to go like 3 metres back from the tip – it was about 10 metres long – and started to slash. It just took one slash. Blood spurted out and I threw the part that was cut away. It spasmed and I gagged.

In retrospect, that was useless, except for putting the thing into temporary pain.

"Let's get away from this," Sarthak panted.

I suddenly gasped. I was feeling a sharp pain near my ribs, and I figured that it was broken. I sat down on the ground and that just made it worse.

Sarthak ran to me. "Are you okay?"

"Do I look okay?" I grimaced.

He helped me up while I whimpered. I was suddenly in a lot of pain. Out of the corner of my eye, I thought I saw something big and red flash by. It left a trail of a shade of red that I couldn't decipher.

"Did you see that?" I asked Sarthak.

"Yeah," he said. "What the hell? It kinda looked like a bird, didn't it?"

It did. I nodded. "We can tell the others later. Right now, run."

He nodded back at me and put his arm around me, helping me walk.

"We need to run, you know," I grimaced."

"I know. We also need your rib to not snap in two pieces, so bear with me."

I gave him a grateful look as we hobbled over to Pari and Yash. The tentacle they had cut off was still throbbing on the ground. Both of them were stained purple and from what little I could see, both of them had looks of disgust on their faces.

"Never imagined I'd *actually* be cutting off space monster tentacles," Yash laughed.

"And it *squirted*," Pari sounded the most disgusted I had ever seen her sound.

"Right, let's stop there," Anita said, making all of jump. "No more details. Let's get out of here."

"Nobody's asking."

She looked at me. "What the hell happened to you?"

"Most probably a broken rib," I said.

"WHAT?" Pari said. "Are you ok?" She came over to help Sarthak.

"Wait," Anita said. She took a bottle out of her backpack and gave it to me. "Drink this and don't move for about a minute. *Definitely* don't sit."

I started to drink and I felt a sharp pain near my ribs. I grimaced and gripped Sarthak and Pari's shoulders. After ten seconds, that pain was gone. I stood still for a minute, and then Anita told me to move around a bit. The pain in my ribs was gone, and I let out a breath. It had literally hurt to breathe.

"Thanks," I said.

"Let's move now," she said. We heard a big screech behind us and something whipping into our direction. It was in Anita's peripheral view, and she blocked it with her dagger. It turned out to be something acidic because the dagger melted. Anita grunted in frustration. That had to require a *lot* of skill.

"*Move*," she literally shouted at us, whipping out a new dagger.

We started to follow her, in what I thought was west, because the sun was setting in our eyes.

We found another flat surface and threw some rocks around in case this was the hiding place of another in case another acid-spitting octopus had decided to nest here.

Anita got the tent out and we got in. From what I could see, it had two rooms, a kitchen and a living room, with two black couches and a fire with a chimney. We were in a frickin hotel suite in the middle of the mountains on a different planet. This tent looked exactly like a hotel room on Earth, so I was pretty sure Anita got to choose it. It was warm inside the tent, and I took my helmet off.

"You can take your external gear off," she told us. "The first room is yours because its bigger, the second one is mine. Don't throw them away because we don't have a lot of extra.

"Who says 'external gear'?" Sarthak said.

"People who don't know what to call all the crap you got on yourselves," Anita said, grimacing at the purple stains on us.

"How are *you* clean?" I suddenly wanted to punch something very bad.

"Years of killing space monsters. Even planetary ones. This one wasn't from here, and that's good."

"Why…?" I said tentatively.

"Because that means we're close. Closer than I expected to be in a day."

"How do you even know where the site for the ritual is?" Yash sounded as frustrated as me.

"It's on the top of the frickin mountain. I don't *need* to know where it is."

"And how do you know that?" Sarthak inquired.

"Sayon was told that by the head of the Fairies. We're pretty sure she wasn't lying, so here we are."

"We're here on a hunch?" Yash said incredulously.

"Yep," Anita replied grimly.

Yash groaned. "So, if the place of the ritual isn't on the peak of this mountain, it's somewhere else?"

"You just said what I said in fewer words," Anita replied.

"I'll go sleep."

The four of us took our coverings off, and I was now just in the clothes Anita had given to me yesterday. The bird suddenly came to my mind, but I decided not to bring that up because the four of us were exhausted. We went to the living room and sat down on the couches. For some time, it felt like we weren't on a mountain where we had almost been eaten by an octopus with acid in its spit. And texture like rock.

"Why doesn't Earth have monsters like these?" I thought out loud.

"You want some of 'em where we live?" Yash was amused.

"Well, no, but I'm just curious. Xinain is obviously a lot like Earth. People are just bigger here. I'm wondering if something like this could have been on our planet too."

"Well, there were dinosaurs," I said. "And I'm pretty sure that the people here would be fascinated by animals on Earth."

He shrugged. "I guess."

Pari took her phone out. "Guys, we got Wi-Fi here."

"Do you wanna call our parents?" Yash asked us.

"You're kidding, right?" I said, flabbergasted.

"Why…?"

"It's your parents that got abducted, dude."

"Oh yeah. Forgot about that. They're probably alright now."

"Did you tell Gertrude about it?"

"Yeah."

Our nonchalance was disturbing.

Sarthak and Pari were on their phones. I liked how quiet it was after our little shenanigan with the octopus thingy. I wondered how Anita knew it wasn't from this planet. I heard a distinct roar outside our tent. The four of us looked up, and Anita came out of her room.

"That doesn't sound very good," she said, and went over to the dining room. There she pulled a weird contraption. It looked like a solenoid with two balls on either side. The four of us burst out laughing when she took it out. She was right. We needed help.

She pulled the spheres out, and a shockwave went around the tent.

"What'd that do?" I asked.

"Made a force field around us," Anita said. "It'll hold for 12 hours. Do not sleep for more than 8 hours because we have to move in approximately 8 hours and 30 minutes to get to the caves."

"Why?" Yash asked her.

"Because why not." Anita refused to elaborate further.

Yash shrugged and started to make his way to our room, and we followed him. The room was simple, with 4 twin-sized beds and a table in the middle. We sat down on the beds and I was almost immediately sleepy. I rested my head on my pillow and fell immediately asleep.

Yash shrugged and started to make his way to our room, and we followed him. The room was simple, with 4 twin-sized beds and a table in the middle. We sat down on the beds and I was almost immediately sleepy. I rested my head on my pillow and fell immediately asleep, thinking about the red bird.

CHAPTER 10

Abduction. Again

We were woken up by Anita, and surprisingly I didn't have a terrible sleep after a long time. My sleep schedule had been pretty much non-existent the last week, and having a good sleep made me realize how tired I had been feeling the past few days. I took a deep breath and took a look around me. Anita was waking everybody up, and basically pushed me out of bed towards the bathroom.

"You're sweaty," was all she said.

I was indeed sweaty, and it felt good to take a shower with nothing on my mind. Except, you know, that we were being forced to do something against our will and that we might possibly die. I was kind of used to that feeling now.

In about half an hour, all of us were ready to go.

"So, where do we go now?" I asked.

"I already told you a million times," Anita said.

My frustration was on the verge of spilling out as destruction. "You didn't tell us nothing."

"And it's gonna stay that way."

"What do you think we'll do if you tell us? Notify earth?" I mocked her, very close to punching her.

Anita gave me a dirty look, and opened the door of our tent. The weather was the same as the last time we were out in the open. I groaned. I didn't feel cold, but looking at the landscape around us, all dreary and a waste, felt depressing. Like I was looking at the thing with no end, and no way out. Kind of like our situation. I clenched my fists.

"Let's move," Anita said, and there was a distant roar over the noise of the blizzard. That had to be the same creature we had ran away from. I hoped we just didn't have to encounter it again.

Anita turned to the four of us, looking kind of like a drill sergeant.

"From this point on, we're gonna be facing a lot of creatures. Always keep your weapons at hand, and be vigilant *all* the time. You relax, you die."

"You're making it sound like a warzone," Yash told her.

"Because it is," Anita cut him off. "We'll have to fight stuff along the way. You realize this right?"

"What is… *stuff*?" Sarthak asked tentatively.

"Well, animals, and the monstrosities like the one we fought before."

"There's *more*?"

"Of course." She said it nonchalantly, like it meant almost nothing.

Fear gripped my heart as the tent collapsed in on itself, and reduced to the size of a laptop. I realized what we were about to face, and it could just be fatal. I found myself not caring. The technological advancements other species had made still amazed me.

"Alright," Anita said, putting the tent in her bag. "We leave now. Please take care."

She said it with what sounded like genuine concern, and I was reminded that the Xinains were not monsters and in fact were fighting for… what?

We started our trek, and I heard another distant roar.

"Was that the same…?" Sarthak. It did seem to be really similar to the creature we had fought.

"No," Anita said. "That is something else, and it is close. Come."

I looked up, looking up at the mountain we were supposed to scale. I saw a glint of red again, but it turned out to be glare from the sun. I was beginning to wonder if that bird was *just* a bird. But it didn't make sense that we hadn't seen a single bird in the time we were here.

There was a rumble as an avalanche shifted on the mountain beside us. I realized that could be us next, and I remembered all the ways to die on a mountain.

"Don't worry, that will not happen to us," Anita yelled over the headset, but it was hard to hear because of the avalanche. "Well, it can, but as long as y'all behind me and within ten metres of me when it's happening, you won't die."

I hated that she said die so nonchalantly, as if people dying was an everyday thing for her. But she was in the field, and had probably been in a warzone, along with other potentially fatal dangers. It probably *was* an everyday thing for her.

We could also be an everyday thing.

The landscape never changed as the hours rolled by. It was just a void beside us, and all white in front of us. it was dead silent except for wind, and nobody was talking. All of us were exhausted, and the eerie quiet of the mountain, most of the wind blocked by the one much larger than this one, gave it such a depressing vibe.

"How much longer until we rest?" I said, not really tired, but I just felt like stopping.

"We can do it right now, but we gotta leave in like 20 minutes," Anita said. "All we will have time for is eating, and I don't think anybody else needs anything else."

As soon as she said that, the fact that I was hungry moved to my conscious mind and I realized my stomach was grumbling. Yash, Pari and Sarthak agreed quickly as Anita set her bag down on the ground. She took the now small tent out and threw it over a flat surface. It expanded, and we went in through the door.

We ate what looked like pizza, but it was a square, with new vegetables and new sauces. Nobody questioned about what it contained, and we wrapped up in 15 minutes.

We got out and Anita grabbed the tent. As soon as the tent collapsed, a 3-metre- long humanoid, black, furry creature erupted out of nowhere and leapt in our general direction. It was thankfully slow, and we were able to get out of range before it jumped into our midst.

"Stay a good distance away from this," Anita said into our headsets, not yelling as if not to alert the creature. "This is a Growler, or as it's called in Xinain, a *Leipeng*, native to this mountain range. It can move short distances very fast, and-"

She started to run backwards as the Leipeng suddenly moved a distance of 10 metre or so in her direction, leaving a short distance between it and us.

We shot at it as we were running backwards, but half our…laser pellets? I didn't know what to call them. Half of our laser pellets went this way and that, but some struck the Leipeng, and it was slowed. It fell down to one knee, and Anita yelled, "Aim at it shoulders and above the thighs!"

She didn't tell us the reason, but we proceeded to obey her. We went back a few metres because it moved closer to us quicker than the eyes. We were lucky it wasn't intelligent, because it was coming in our general direction and not targeting one person.

It let out an ear-splitting roar, as one of its legs fell off. There was blood, but the creature's body quickly covered that. There was a surprisingly pleasant smell that wafted across to us, and I was both fascinated and disgusted. It was almost like the smell was a reward for killing it.

"Leave!" Anita yelled.

We started to turn away from the creature, as it groaned in agony. With each agony-afflicted groan, we heard the creature dying. I winced at every one of them.

Soon, we were away from the Leipeng and making our way up the mountain again. We faced no dangers as we got to our destination, and Anita opened up the tent.

I sat down on a nearby rock. "I'm not tired," I said. "How?"

Sarthak, and Yash were out of their breath. Pari had spent the last hour talking to me, and we hadn't realized when we had reached our destination.

As soon as Anita kept the tent on the ground, there was a shriek above us. Anita picked up the tent as something that looked like a small fireball rained down on us.

"Fire hawks!" Anita shouted. She didn't say what they were called in Xinain, but it was enough to make us scatter like insects.

There was a big, white bird about 30 metres above us, flying swiftly around us, and shooting badly aimed fireballs.

"How do we fight this?" Sarthak yelled. "Why are there so many weird animals here? Where are these things on Earth?"

"There's strong magical presence here," Anita replied while running. "Magic left undisturbed damages the ecological balance. Animals change."

Another small fireball landed near me. It was really near me, but I didn't feel heat.

"One of them is not a problem," Anita said, as we turned to run below a crevice. "If there's a hoard of them, we're gonna get injured badly."

Oh my god, I thought. *Fire is gonna hurt. No way!*

I decided not to say this out loud.

As the bird forgot about us, we got out of the crevice and went up the mountain, back to our spot where Anita had opened up the tent. We were not *completely* exhausted, and before I knew it, all of us were in our room on the beds and were dead asleep.

In what was probably the morning, Anita barged into our room and told us to get ready. "We reach our destination today. We'll do the ritual tomorrow."

"This quick?" I asked her in confusion.

"Well, you see, our detour due to the Leipeng gave way to a new, shorter path, which wasn't supposed to exist, but apparently it does."

It all sounded too convenient to me, and Anita sounded dubious while saying it. We really had no choice since going back to where the Leipeng attacked us would be quite the ordeal.

"If the path doesn't in fact exist, we will go back to our old spot and then it'll take us an extra week to get to the ritual place."

'Ritual place' sounded so sacred and important. I realized we could face serious damage at that ritual place. Sayon had assured us that it wouldn't be fatal, but I had my doubts.

We took the tent with us and left the place.

We reached the top of the mountain surprisingly early.

It was the wrong top.

The four of us were looking accusatorily at Anita, who seemed confused. She was mumbling to herself. "But the compass… it pointed to this location right here… I don't get it… how?"

She was ignoring us for the time being, and I decided that there was nothing we could really do except going down the mountain and going up the right one.

But there seemed to be no mountains in our close midst. They were at the edge of our vision, and *quite* far.

"This has to be the right mountain," Anita said to herself more than to us. "We're just at the wrong place." She sounded like she was on the edge of a panic attack.

There was a *zhing* noise as a portal materialized right next to us, and engulfed us.

I gasped for air as we found ourselves in a small, grey metal chamber, with what appeared to be no escape.

"W-what?" I spoke.

All 5 of us were disoriented, and nobody answered my question, because obviously they didn't know the answer.

"What the hell happened?" Yash said.

"How would we know?" Sarthak said, voicing my thoughts.

Anita sat up groggily and looked around, probably assessing the situation. The situation, by her expression, was bad and she was just as clueless as we were.

The chamber opened up, and we found ourselves in what looked like… the ship we had been in when we were rescued from that Xinain compound.

I heard a familiar bark as Striker jumped onto us. Elation filled me as I realized that we were back with Gertrude and Glenda.

"You're back!" Gertrude yelled, and enveloped the four of us in a hug.

She then noticed Anita, and backed off.

"Who's this?" Gertrude was apprehensive.

We started to tell her the whole story as men came and restrained Anita. She didn't protest, and neither did we as we were so happy.

After we were finished, I decided to state the obvious. "How did you find us?"

"We were able to pinpoint the location due to the ship, and just needed to find a source of heat. No technology really made it harder for us, but you're here!" Gertrude clapped her hands, looking like a kid.

I was only kinda happy that we were back with them. The fact that we had escaped only meant Sayon would come back for us, and she would probably get her way, with these weird portals. It was making my head hurt, and frankly, I just wanted to go home.

"I wanna go home," I groaned, and none of the others protested.

"We are taking you home," Gertrude answered me in a soft voice, "After this war is over. Before that, nobody's going nowhere. The threat of Hanginton still hangs loose, but I don't think she cares about you now."

"How is the war going anyway?" I asked her like it was a TV show, but I just didn't seem to care anymore. I was tired and frustrated, because one thing kept leading to next. I never wanted to see the Hangintons' or the Tiaras' faces ever again. "Are actual people fighting them?"

"No, they're way past that," Gertrude said, laughing. "The supposed battleground is just a wasteland of broken machines. Literal *millions* of tonnes of iron and other things. It makes me sad."

"Well, it is better than loss of lives, no?" Yash asked.

"I guess it is, but not in the long run." It was dark, but that was kind of the truth.

"Who's winning?" Pari asked her.

"Nobody," Gertrude answered. "This war is probably gonna end in a stalemate, and the Whizari and Namerians are going to sign a peace treaty."

"What about the Marsians?"

"They're just a pawn in this power grab."

"Power over who?" I chimed in.

"Resources, reputation in the galaxy, etc."

I was pretty sure she was dumbing it down for us since it couldn't be that simple, but we decided to end the discussion as the General came in.

He nodded at us and said, "Welcome back."

"Thanks," the four of us chanted in unison.

"So, we have found out a way for you to get out without getting intercepted," he started. "But it is kind of long, and not to mention inaccurate and may land you 10 miles from where you live. Is that what you use in all countries? It's too confusing for me."

If any of us gave a damn about being dropped 10 kilometres away, they could stay here for all I cared.

"Any of you got a problem?" I asked them, not expecting no as an answer.

Sarthak looked a little reluctant to go back yet, but nobody protested. I guess all of us were tired of the commotion and needed the calm.

The General beamed. "Ok then," he started to walk towards a door, and told us to follow. "Follow me."

I turned to Gertrude. "Are you coming with us?"

"Nope," she said. "I'll be back with Glenda."

I sighed. "Why?"

"She's kinda a friend who I was enemies with for a long time. I wanna spend some time with her, and there is kinda a war where I could help out." Gertrude trying to talk like teenagers was hilarious.

"Yeah," I said. I was kind of sad that I probably wouldn't see Gertrude for a long time. We had just met.

As we started to leave the room, waving goodbye to Gertrude, the General led us into a small ship the size of a small room. It was connected to the ship we were on by a thing that looked like an aerobridge, the stuff that connected airplanes to the airport. As soon as the door of the ship closed, I heard the thing retracting back into the ship.

Inside the ship, it was simple. There were 6 beds, a T.V. and some charging ports.

"Are we gonna be the only ones in here?" I asked the General.

"Yes," he replied. "The ship needs to go to a beacon, because directly Portalling from here will send out its location, and mark this ship as hostile, in which case it would get blown out of the air. To get to the beacon, however, you require 1 day. This ship cannot get intercepted, so do not worry, you are safe. The path has already been mapped, and in case of some stray asteroids, there's cannons on this ship."

I had an urge to as him "Who asked" but since this was our ticket out of here, I decided to keep my mouth shut.

The General started to walk towards the door and pressed a button. I heard the same noise I had heard while the bridge was retracting. There was a small bang as the door opened and the General walked out the ship.

"The food is in the back," he said. "Lot of Earth *and* Marsian things so enjoy yourselves, ever-hungry teens." He said it with the air of trying to be cool, but it was so funny the four of us burst laughing the moment he was out of earshot. The door closed and the ship started to move. There was a low humming as the ship burst into full speed.

"I guess we got nothing to do for a day?" Yash voiced out all of our thoughts.

"I *really* hope this place has Wi-Fi." Pari immediately went to check on her phone.

She groaned.

"Then we just watch T.V., I guess?" I said, disappointed.

We tried to turn the T.V on, but it wasn't gonna.

Sarthak cursed. "What do we do?"

"Sit around I guess," I sighed.

As soon as I said that, our ship stuttered to a stop.

"What in the-?" I swore.

An alarm in our ship sounded as it started to go off its path. I was now on the verge on crying, because I was promised this was over. I wanted out. I wanted to go home.

I sat down as our ship docked into something, and I waited for the men that came in through the doors to grab me.

We were sedated and carried into what looked like a prison cell, with 5 stools. 4 of them were occupied by the 4 of us, and 1 sat empty.

"This was supposed to be over," Sarthak groaned. "Weren't we supposed to be nontrackable or something? Who got us?"

"I think it's pretty obvious who did." The door had opened and a woman all of us hated with all our hearts was standing in the doorway.

Soundleek Hanginton stood in the doorway.

"Long time no see, huh?" she said.

It was ironic, considering we would have been safer if we had gone back to earth.

I remembered what we used to call her: *O-wash*. The cringe it carried made me want to throw up. What were we thinking? Why did it seem like a good name? I had forgotten the full form to that, and I was glad.

"To answer your obvious question, I am alive because of necromancy," she laughed, and I realized it was a joke.

"Your sense of humour hasn't got better, from what I can see," Yash snickered.

Soundleek glared at him. "Be glad I cannot kill you on the spot."

That meant she knew about our magic, and was here because of it.

"Are you gonna take us back to the Xinains?" Pari asked her.

"Hell no," she scoffed, "Who would go back to those fools?"

This kept getting worse. This probably meant that Hanginton was going to use us for her magic for something that would *not* be very good for the world. I itched to mock her about this, but she actually looked angry right now.

"Let's go, then," she said. She snapped her finger, and a guy in a suit that looked similar to the ones they had worn when they had attacked us when we were with Hamilton, came in with a box about the size of a shoebox. It was blue, with what seemed like a black pearl studded in the centre. It gave off a strong scent of something I couldn't tell, but it was definitely something I had smelled before.

As the man set down the box, the scent only spread, and I remembered where I had smelt it before.

The Leipeng's blood.

I remembered Anita telling us that it was native to that specific mountain range, and I wondered if we were going to go to the place we had originally meant to go to. I was kind of curious to see what it was, but at the same time, we were probably going to die now, since Hanginton would have no use for us after she had our magic. The thought scared me to death. I wished it would stay figurative.

As time went on, none of us spoke. A portal started to materialize at the place of the small box. This was about my height, which meant it was not very tall, and it was dark blue. A small glow emerged from it, lighting up the otherwise dark room. I wondered who had killed the lights, or they had gone out automatically due to the no technology restrictions in the place of the ritual. We hadn't been told what it was called, so I intended to keep calling it the ritual place.

The portal opened up fully, and through the swirling curtain of purple, I could see a mountain range, and a slope of mountain that kept going on as far as I could see.

We were pushed through the portals after being handed identical gear to the clothes we had worn when we were with Anita. The wind was strong, and we had difficulty walking. There was a gaping chasm in front of us.

As far as the eye could see, sharp, grey rock stretched on and on. I could not contemplate how bad of a calamity it had to be to create this, and I wondered if it was natural or magical. When I looked down into it, my hands bound, I could not see the bottom, but what I did smell was a *much* stronger version of the smell of the Leipeng we had encountered.

"What's down there?" I asked Hanginton.

"Why should I answer you?" she said, her nostrils flaring like a five-year-old.

My friends and I snickered at her. She looked enraged and proceeded to tell us. "It is the place where a lot of Leipengs reside, and feed on each other. You do *not* wanna be down there."

"No way," Yash said. "Thank you for telling us we do not wanna be in a place full of things that would kill us."

Hanginton looked like a mother that was tired of her teenage kids, which worked out because she was around the age of my mom. She looked like she wanted to throw one of us down the chasm. And knowing what she was capable of, she would do it even if it affected her adversely.

The growls of the Leipengs chilled my spine. Or that was just the cold. Either way, the air around us was very hostile. Nobody spoke a word as we crossed a bridge Hanginton's men had laid out for us. It looked fragile, as if wind could break it, but when we got on it, it didn't creak once. It was blue in colour. As we crossed, I got a closer look into the chasm. What I saw didn't sit well in my stomach.

Hordes of Leipengs leapt on each other, fighting. Apparently, their only food source was accessible through cannibalism. I could see so many splotches of red on the white snow, and the sickening-sweet smell we had encountered when we had crippled the Leipeng made me want to throw up. It was way stronger than it had been when we were at the edge of the chasm. I wanted to throw up, but the plank was just about a foot wide for some reason.

I looked down again, where the chasm got deeper, and I saw that a small riverine flowing in the corner of the ravine like a gutter, and it did seem to clean up the cliff; by a very little amount, and it just made way for insects and smell. I let in a deep breath as soon as we crossed the chasm, which was a mistake, because the smell hadn't gotten better. I threw up on Hanginton's shoes, and my friends burst into laughter.

"One more time you piss me off," she said, with violence in her eyes, "You're gonna be Leipeng-fodder.

That sounded very funny the way she said it, and it was unfamiliar to us, so we burst out laughing. She took in a deep breath as if to regulate her heartbeat.

I realized these were probably the last moment of our lives, so why not make it better?

"We have two hours of trekking ahead of us," Hanginton said. "If u want to talk, do it away from me. I am already too annoyed."

We waited back a little until she was out of earshot.

"Ok, we need to think," Sarthak said.

"You have handcuffs on your hand," Pari said. "There's so no thinking our way out of this one. We have always had our butts saved by either Gertrude or Glenda or *somebody*. This time, I'm not so positive." Her voice sounded on the verge of tears.

Due to her words, I realized the magnitude of the situation. We weren't going back to our parents unless a miracle occurred.

I suddenly remembered the headphones Anita had given to us, but my excitement died down quickly as I remembered that I had thrown it away when we had been rescued.

"Any of you got the headphones Anita had given to us?" I said quietly just in case. They seemed taken aback.

"Yeah, but they're under the clothes I'm wearing under these," Pari said excitedly, a glint of hope in her eyes shining through the terror and sadness. I realized this thought made me sound like some 80-year-old author. I didn't know why I thought it was a bad thing. "I can't take it off here, they're gonna notice."

"No way! Really?" Yash exclaimed.

She cast him a dirty look, and since she looked on the verge of tears, Yash decided to shut up. Her lower lip trembled, and Sarthak rubbed her shoulder. I wondered what was happening to her.

"What are you doing?" I said to her, and it might have come off as confrontational.

She just sighed. "We're gonna die. I don't know what's happening to me, but I sure as hell don't wanna die."

This sounded ridiculous, but we decided to keep out mouths shut. Of course, I didn't wanna die. I guess she was just scared.

I realized how messed up my thinking was right now. Of *course,* she was afraid. We were about to *die.* Even though there was a very small chance that we would be rescued through Anita's headphone's help, it took a very heavy toll on me.

"It's alright," Sarthak said eventually.

Hanginton shouted at us. "Walk faster!"

We did not, indeed, walk faster.

The ritual place was magnificent.

Among the rocks, with the backdrop of the blue sky, and clouds making it all a hazy mess, we could see the black and for some reason *orange* ruins of what looked like a temple. I wondered if the person who had designed this place was colourblind, because black and bright *orange* looked like someone had puked rainbows. But just orange.

Somebody took a deep breath, and instinct made me do the same. I didn't know how, but the air was somehow *different* here. Like it was infused with magic.

It probably literally *was* infused with magic.

The view was breathtakingly beautiful, I had to admit. But I did wonder what kind of magic or what kind of ritual needed to be performed on us for this to be the place that we had to travel to.

As we got closer, I realized the place wasn't actually in ruins, it was just built that way. It looked like its construction was incomplete, and it had apparently been carved from rock. Maybe the people who chiselled this had got bored. I wondered why my thoughts were messed up.

"The walk up to it will take some time," Hanginton said. "About 30 minutes."

Her words made me realize that the place was humongous. I looked to Pari and gave her a perplexed look.

"How big *is* that thing?" Yash whispered.

I wanted to reply with sarcasm, but Sarthak beat me to it, comparing it with the size of something else.

Hanginton glared back at us. She looked like she wanted to kill us then and there. She had that look permanently, so it didn't make a difference.

After 15 minutes, the slope we were climbing ended, and it was just rock that we now had to walk on to get to the… *rock.*

"What the hell is it called?" I asked Hanginton.

"Nothing," she replied. "Anybody alive who knows about this place includes the people here, and those two idiots." I assumed she was talking about Sayon and Anita.

"*What*?" Sarthak said. "There has to be someone who knew. Who told all of *you*?"

"I did say they had to be alive," Hanginton said. "You have to thank me for it."

There was silence. No one said a word as we trudged the rocks, making our way to the ritual place. In the corner of my eye, I saw a glint of red.

CHAPTER 11

Ooh Frosty

That couldn't be a coincidence. How many bizarre phoenix-like birds existed, that looked like it left a trail of fire? Apparently, people around me saw it too, and everybody turned to the bird. It wasn't very high up in the air. I could probably throw a rock at it. I had a very bad perception of distances, so I couldn't tell if it was 15 metres or 50.

"That is so big," Yash said. He realized what his words sounded like, and the four of us burst out laughing.

"I just can't with you people's humour," Hanginton muttered.

But if the bird was big, it meant that it was very far away and I could not indeed throw a rock at it.

"Just move," Pari said. "We're close anyways. The bird doesn't matter."

But her voice made me feel like it did matter. She didn't sound as depressed she had been before, and this wasteland of rocks had given us all the more reason to act that way. I hoped she had a plan, because I was starting to feel hopeless myself.

After some time, we were at the steps of what led to the ruins. The steps were about 4 feet tall, and there were about 20 of them. We started to climb them, pushing ourselves up the way we would go over a fence. After doing that about 10 times, I was pretty exhausted, and so were the others. The thin air did not help. I gestured to my friends to stop, and Sarthak called for a break. Hanginton seemed out of breath too.

After some time, we started to climb again. Excruciatingly, I made myself go over the last one, and collapsed on the ground. I looked to my right, and a magnificent sight met my eyes.

Three spires rose out of the main structure, and the one in the middle was the tower. It had to be more than 200 metres in breadth, and it was *tall*. I had seen the Kanchenjunga, albeit from a distance, but I knew what *very* tall meant. This crossed that limit. From below the stairs, the other two spires had been clouded by, well, *clouds*, and we hadn't been able to make them out. 32

"How was this made?" I said, taking a breath in before each word.

"Magical accident," one of the people from Hanginton's crew replied.

Hanginton interrupted him, giving him a dangerous look. "Fairies were trying to use the same magic you have in your veins. They chose the wrong place for it. It consumed all of their power *and* them, and this place made itself. They were using this place so that they could store the power into a magical artifact, and this was the perfect place for it since it was the resting place of a mythical sword. Instead, they got this hellhole and that ice on the top the place of that magic. We break the ice, the magic is released, I store it. Then I extract yours."

"Why can't you just take it without the magic?" I asked.

"The magic in you is attracted to the ice, so it will be easier not losing it," she replied.

"Why not just use the ice?" Yash asked.

"Anybody who uses that magic, dies."

"*What*?"

Hanginton sighed in exasperation. "No mortal body will be able to take the brunt of the Ice on the Tower."

That was a bad name. Yash's thoughts reverberated mine. "That's a bad name."

"That's the name *I* gave it," Hanginton said, and the four of us sniggered. I wondered what had got into us. We were facing what would probably be the last few hours of our life, but I guess having somebody save our butts every time incited these reactions. We had to do something this time, because I was sure Hanginton had taken every possible precaution this time, since us getting out of these situations had become a given. We ended our break and started to move.

We were almost at the Tower. I could see the ice on it very clearly, and I wondered why the magic had chosen a random clump of ice to store its entirety. It was impractical, but I doubted undirected magic had brains. It was still strange. And the air here seemed… *denser*. I guess this was what Anita had meant by no technology.

We finally arrived at the doorway.

"What, do we knock now?" Sarthak asked, and I doubted if it was even sarcastic.

We heard a guttural roar from inside the Tower. I had decided to call the whole structure the Tower, because it was easier, and I really didn't have any brains left over.

My heart clenched in fear as if whatever we had heard inside had been right next to us.

It was as if the creatures heard my thoughts.

There was a yelp from one of Hanginton's men as a wolf like creature emerged and pounced on him. He staggered back, and managed to shake the wolf off. It had to be 2 metres long, but it was taller than most of us, towering a metre or more above us. It was a handsome animal, with a fur coat that looked like it would enclose all of me, its face twisted into a snarl. It reared back on its hind legs, let out a guttural roar similar to the one we had heard from inside the Tower, and leapt onto the man again. It was shot down, but the man had a wound on his arm.

It screeched a little and rolled over, its eyes lifeless. It twitched a little, but was completely still a little while later. I looked over at my friends, and gulped. They looked like they had peed their pants, and it was probably the same for me.

Yash swore. "What the hell is that?"

Hanginton started walking towards the door again. "They're the guardians of the temple. I thought the Leipengs had killed them off, but apparently not."

"Could there be Leipengs *inside* that thing?" I whispered.

"A lot of maybes," was all Hanginton said.

She took out something that looked like a miniature bazooka, instructed us to cover our years, and blew out a small hole just big enough to get us in, into the door of the Tower with a deafening bang. Even with my ears covered, it felt like my eardrums had been blown in. My ears ringing, and a fearful look on everybody's face, we walked into the Tower.

Inside, not a thing was visible. An eerie feeling settled onto my stomach, and I felt like this would be a good starting to a horror movie. Hanginton took a torch out and lit up the space around us, but it seemed to be of no use because we could not see anything except for each other's faces. It felt unbelievably hot in there, and one of Hanginton's men told us to take our coverings off. We did, and with a whirring noise, they folded themselves into a box the size of a paper weight. There were sighs of relief, and I walked closer to my friends. I wondered why it was so hot in here. Magic was weird.

"We have to split up," Hanginton said. I wondered if she said it on purpose. My heart was beating so loud I was sure everybody in a 10-metre radius would have been able to hear it.

She sniggered. "You should have seen your faces."

I wanted to punch her.

"We have to find a flight of stairs," she said. She started handing out torches similar to hers, but of less magnitude.

"Just make sure you do not break something, and don't wander into any doorways. You will feel fatigue more than usual due to this crap magic, but do not worry."

The door behind us repaired itself with a *shink*.

"Well, since y'all have nowhere to run, go crazy," she told us. Was she growing softer? I wanted to say that to her but I didn't wanna ruin our chances of surviving.

Me and my friends started to walk into a random direction, and Pari whispered, "Do you… *feel* different? Like, not fatigue, but I feel *energetic*."

Her words made me realize that I indeed did feel like I could run a marathon right now. For some reason, being exposed to the magic inside the temple had not tired us, but it was helping us.

"Has to be our magic, right?" Yash said uncertainly.

"Has to be," Pari whispered.

"Can we *use* it?" Sarthak stated the obvious question that had to have been in Yash's and Pari's brain.

"How do you suggest we do that, exactly?" Pari's voice was laced with heavy sarcasm.

"I don't know. Feel it?"

There was laughter.

"Let's focus on finding the staircase, ok?" I shut them up. "We'll figure things along as we go."

They agreed with me, and we started to move around. We decided to hold hands to not get lost.

"I feel like a kid," Yash grumbled.

"We got torches, you idiots," Sarthak muttered, and broke his hand away from me. The four of us stayed close.

The silence between us and the darkness in the Tower was eerie. I felt like anything could come at us any moment and tear us to shreds, just like the soldier had been.

We put one hand on a wall and came across a weird contraption near our legs. It looked like someone had dumped a random battery here with no connections whatsoever.

I kicked it and the lights came on. They were so high up; it was a wonder the room was as bright as it was. I looked up and saw and it was like looking at the sun.

Hanginton shouted in delight, then saw that I had done it. She sniggered then. "You just fast-forwarded your death."

I really didn't care about her threats now. I was almost sure that we would make it out of here. I wasn't going down without a fight anyways. I didn't know *what* I would be fighting with, but I would be fighting.

We found the staircase we were looking for nearly 15 minutes later, tucked into a room nearly 100 metres away from the hall we had been searching. There was no way in hell we would have found the staircase out without me turning the lights on. The room was plain, just grey like the rest of the Tower. The blandness of colour made me want to kick something, because the sight wasn't pretty to my eyes. That and the fact that this whole thing had been a hell hole. But the lights were more annoying. There were no runes, no decorations, no torches, just that weird sun-like light that seemed to be visible from everywhere.

"Really shouldn't have turned that crap on," Sarthak whispered.

"Yeah," Pari said, and laughed, which was a good sign. At least she was back to humour, even though it was a crappy joke. I was worried about her, but we had had no time talk, I had had no time to listen to her. I really wanted to know what was going on with her.

The staircase went to the top of the tower, and there was what would be a humongous door when we got to it at the end of it. Craning up my neck, I tried to estimate how tall the Tower was. I couldn't. It was just too big, way bigger than the Burj Khalifa or anything tall I had ever seen. That was counting Himalayan mountains. The trek up the stairs would not be fun, to say the least. My friends had awestruck looks on their faces that replicated mine. There was comparatively lesser light here, and I noticed the sun had stopped following us.

"Alright," Hanginton said. "Obviously I didn't know there was a Godzilla-sized staircase that led to the top, so we're gonna be taking breaks as we go along. We should be reaching in 3-4 days, and I don't think there's gonna be anything we're gonna have to fight."

I highly doubted that, but I appreciated the optimism. Then I realized that I was appreciating Hanginton, and instantly talked crap about her to my friends.

We started up the staircase. There's really nothing to say about going up identical stairs endlessly.

I wondered how something of this magnitude had been created as a mistake. No rock was carved like this without a prerequisite thought. At least, I thought. No way a being similar to humans on earth were this powerful, right? But I didn't have a perception of what people could handle, so I couldn't really say.

My thoughts dragged on an on as my feet did the same. After about climbing over stairs for about an hour at the speed of a snail, Hanginton called for a break.

We ate something that looked like an energy bar, which tasted bland. But my hunger disappeared, so I was content. I also felt a fresh rush of energy, like somebody had just drugged me. Knowing Hanginton, that was possible. But right now, I didn't care about anything that would be detrimental to my long-term health. I worried I wasn't going to live up to another week.

My thoughts sluggish due to the constant… just *everything*. I was exhausted; not physically. I was tired of running after stuff, and I was sure every one of my friends was too.

The three days were over.

And so were the ways where we could go.

At the end of the staircase, we had just run into a dead end. There was nowhere to go. The wall in front of us, in its grey glory, rose for about 50 metres before curving inwards into a dome.

All of us were stumped.

"Isn't the ice supposed to be outside?" I whispered to Yash.

He gestured for me to shut up.

Hanginton's face was priceless. She looked like someone had just ripped her favourite weapon to pieces. At least, that's what I imagined a bad thing was for her. This was comedic relief to my brain, and I calmed down a little. But I couldn't help but wonder if we had made it all the way here for nothing.

I walked to Pari and took her hand. Her hand was shaking. I pulled her a little close, and it didn't seem to calm her down.

"Why are you panicking at the best moment?" I whispered to her.

She looked at me like I had lost my mind. "How is this in any way the best moment?" Honestly, I didn't know myself.

She was interrupted by a howl from what seemed to be inside that wall. All of us veered back in shock as a wolf stuck its snout out from the supposedly solid wall. One soldier shot it, but it did nothing to it, and it came out and jumped on top of him. Two more people got down to help him, and threw the wolf down the staircase. We heard its howl as it went down the chasm of the staircase. This name was better than ice on the tower.

CHAPTER 12

The Ice on the Tower

All of us waited, looking at the wall in anticipation of more wolves. It was dead silence as nothing else came out of the walls. The howls behind had stopped too.

Hanginton went over to the wall the wolf had come from, and touched it with her hand. She ran it down the wall, and then, with a little force, threw herself against the wall. She was trying to get into where the wolf came from. I doubted it would be that easy, and after a few futile tries, she stopped trying. She grunted in frustration as she came back to the group.

"Blow it up," she said.

As the four of us watched in shock, some of her soldiers took out double sided tape and stuck some weird looking contraptions onto the walls. There was a square in the middle with a hole the size of a tennis ball, and about two inches above it floated what looked like a tennis ball. The soldiers strapped it, told everybody to step back, and Hanginton pressed a button. The balls fit into the disk, and a deafening boom resounded, me and my friends having no time to cover our ears.

Our ears ringing, I was reminded of Sarthak's ears ringing and him calling it '*TING*' noise. I couldn't believe that was a year ago. And the fact that I remember it so clearly.

The wall was not damaged in the least, but *electricity* sparks ran over the thing for a few seconds before fading away. Either we were lied to, or something weird happened.

"What…?" Hanginton whispered, and the touched the wall tentatively with her hand again.

Her hand swooped in.

She turned to us, smirking. "Get the hell in."

The four of us, followed by the guards, went in.

We were in a small chamber, and it was very dark. The light came from an unknown source. I bumped into one of the walls and saw that the walls were the ones emitting the light.

Hanginton was confused. "What is this?" I wanted to make a snarky remark, but couldn't think of one. Don't judge me.

The chamber started to shake as if it was an earthquake, and I gripped what I thought was Pari's hand. We fell to our feet, and I noticed that Hanginton was gone. In fact, everybody except the four of us were gone from the chamber. I also realized it was getting lighter. The *walls* got brighter. I couldn't see what color they were because of that light. We were now on the ground because the shaking was too much to handle.

None of us said anything as the chamber continued to shake for the better part of the minute. As soon as it stopped, we got up on our feet and the chamber disappeared. I breathed in sharply.

We were in a desolate landscape. As far as my eye could see, there was no vegetation, no rocks. Just plain, grey ground. In the distance we could see smoke billowing from something that looking like a tower.

"That's it," I whispered.

The others looked at me, and I pointed. They realized what I meant.

"How do we get there?"

"We walk, jackass," Sarthak said, starting towards it. We scrambled behind him.

"Why is it just the four of us?" Yash said what everybody was thinking. He was getting pretty good at that lately.

"Magic?" Pari was doubtful. She still looked like a depressed woman in her twenties.

"It's obviously magic, what are you on?"

"No, I mean the magic in *us*," she replied.

I hadn't even remembered that fact, despite the fact that we were in this hellhole *because* we had that magic.

"Maybe you're right," Sarthak said out of nowhere. He had been way ahead of us, and seemed to have run back to catch up to us.

"When the hell did you get here?" Yash asked him.

He was confused. "I literally walked."

We decided to let it go. Things weren't making sense, and maybe this… realm? was making our thought process and our perception of the real world foggy. I was feeling groggy, and my steps were straying away from their path.

"Guys," Yash said like he was high. "I don't feel that good."

And promptly fell to the ground.

My vision got dark.

For the millionth time, we were trapped in a chamber with no door. I would call this fiasco "Chambers with no Doors". The Ice on the Tower was a better name than that atrocity. I scrunched my face and moved on.

Yash groaned lightly as he rubbed his neck. He had been propped up weirdly against the wall, his neck at an odd angle. Sarthak was spreadeagled in a corner. He was snoring. The man was *snoring*.

Yash walked over to him and kicked him lightly in an unpleasant place. Sarthak didn't budge. Yash was about to do it harder until Sarthak shifted around a little. Yash kicked him on his butt. He woke up with a welp.

"What's your prob- Where the hell are we?" he said drowsily.

"Another small goddamn room," Yash said, frustrated. I looked around the room and realized something.

"Where's Pari?" Sarthak and Yash looked around in a frenzy, and soon enough it was clear she wasn't with us in the chamber. It was clear from the start, but our brains took some time to register that.

I was full-on panicking now. "Where'd they take her? Why'd they take her?" and iterations of this nonsense. Sarthak and Yash were as worried as me. Eventually, we calmed down, telling ourselves that she was alright. But it was hard to believe.

"Let's calm down," Sarthak said, "And figure out what the hell we need to do."

"Oh, you don't need to do anything," a pleasant voice with a *weird* English accent came through a speaker that had not been there a moment before. "Just wait. Your friend is with us, and all of you will be too. Don't you worry."

The speaker disappeared. We were dumbstruck. The way that man had said it was obviously meant to creep us out, but I wondered how in an abandoned castle there security like this could be. And a portal to another place or something. Hanginton had not done her homework. Nor had the Xinains. *Homework* was the wrong term for this. They had just… *assumed* what was going to be in the Tower? I scoffed internally.

Yash sat down in a corner, dejected. "Now what?"

"We can't do crap, dude," Sarthak, who was sitting beside him, replied. "We can just wait."

And wait we did. After what seemed like days, some food came in through some non-existential opening in the container. They were burritos. Our space aliens had sent us burritos. I didn't wonder about it much and wolfed it down.

"Ok, now we know wherever we have got Burger King," Sarthak said.

Yash and I cringed. "Ew."

"It wasn't that bad."

"It was."

He shrugged.

I let out a loud groan randomly after a few minutes. It had been really silent. Sarthak and Yash jumped. I snickered a little.

The speaker appeared, and the three of us sat up, hearing the slight *shink*.

"Get out," was all the voice said.

The doors of the chamber opened up around us. A sight met us that we wouldn't have expected in any world.

We were in what looking like a corporate building. It had about six to seven floors, and none of them had railings. And no people. It was just us in a building, a very *big* building. Even though it just had 7 floors, it humongous, just like everything we had seen. It was as if some other creatures had made it, someone way bigger than us. It wouldn't be impossible for that to happen, and I didn't wanna face it.

The floor was completely empty, just one big escalator in the distance. Our footsteps echoed, and it was "HELLO?" Yash shouted in the loudest voice he could possibly ever muster, scaring the crap out of us.

Sarthak smacked him on the head. Yash was pissed and hit him back. Before they could get into a full-on fight and I could get some entertainment, the voice yelled out, "STOP! Go straight to the fountain."

I was about to ask what fountain, but right before our eyes, was a fountain. It had a bowl in the middle on the stand. We had to walk a little before we got to it. Sarthak decided to put his hand into the water and pulled it out.

"It's slimy!" he said, disgusted, trying to get the goop off his hand. When it was finally off, his hand was *very* pale.

"I can't feel it," he whispered. He flopped it around and his fingers moved at odd angles, as if he was shaking clothes.

He cursed. "What is this?"

"It removes your bones," the voice droned, but we couldn't tell from where it was coming. "Now can you all please step into the fountain. I am counting down to one. Whoever's not in will be killed."

Deciding not to call any bluffs, we stepped into the goop. My legs went out from under me. I fell onto my back. My elbows couldn't hold me above the goop, so I went under and stopped feeling anything. I could think, but I couldn't move, I couldn't speak. I could hear though, and it didn't feel like I was underwater. If anything, I could hear clearer.

I could still see, but it was weird. I could see everything in two slightly different parts, like the same movie playing on two screens, but the screens were tilted away from each other.

I mentally screamed. I could see my eyeball looking back at me. I wanted to close my eyes, but my eyelids weren't working. I felt disgust in every bit of my weird body. I moved a bit after trying, and finally managed to look away from my eyeball, towards my arms. They were twice as long, but still as thick. It was very weird to me.

I heard a splash, and saw Pari's clothes, and a dilapidated human being that looked a lot like her. She was dumped in, and then everything blacked out, just after I got the feeling of momentary relief.

I woke up with no feeling in any part of my body, tied to a chair in different clothes. I saw a brown mark that went all around my wrist like a bracelet. I saw it on my other hand too. I wondered if that was to stay, because that stuff was going to look horrible in any outfit available on earth. It was dark brown, an unpleasant color because it looked like poop.

I tried to speak and move my arm, but I felt the same feeling I had while we were in the goop, but this time we were just on chairs instead of floating in goop. I was glad to see Pari was beside us, wide awake. Since we couldn't talk and couldn't express anything, I couldn't ask her where she had been taken.

I could hear talking outside, and that was when I really focused on the room. The walls were bright green for a change. There seemed to be no door. It had windows with blinds like a normal room, but behind the blinds I could only see a faint blue what-looked-like-a-sky. I had a suspicion it wasn't a sky and just a blue screen, but before I could think anymore, a three feet tall woman walked into the room through the wall.

"Hello," she said in that same accented way the voice that had got us here had been in. "How the hell did you get in here?"

We obviously couldn't answer, and she laughed. "Just kidding. That fool Hanginton thought she could get the better of us." She started laughing maniacally at that cliché statement.

"I'm sure you're wondering who I am. Well too bad, because you're never gonna know."

She walked over to Sarthak, picked up what looked like a metal bar, and struck him in the face with it. He bled. I was sure he didn't feel anything, but that scar on his face would remain for some time.

"This is fun," she said. "I don't have to hear everybody's scream."

She walked over to me, who was next to Sarthak. She smacked me on the back of my head. I felt airy, and realized blood came out. Next, she went to Pari, who was already worn out. "Oh, this one had an unfortunate experience. I'm gonna leave you alone."

Her hands suddenly flew to her throat, which was glowing.

And the light was coming out of the four of us. The source seemed to be located where our hearts were. The force of whatever was coming out of us sent the woman flying. She crashed into a wall with a loud bang.

What the hell?

She grunted in disgust. "Oh, you're gonna regret that."

She took out a small bottle from her pocket, and poured it in all of our mouths. I could feel again. I realized why she was doing this. Make us feel again, make us feel the pain again. The woman before us was a monster.

Somehow by some miracle, the back of my head didn't hurt much. I just felt the blood matting in my hair. Blood didn't seem to be flowing anymore.

The woman walked to Pari again. Before she could do it, she was on the ground. Pinned there by Sarthak, who had appeared in the fraction of a second.

I was beginning to realize that maybe this magic inside us was now active. We could actually get the hell out of here.

Sarthak looked like he wanted to do that same thing with the metal bar, but instead he went to Yash and Pari and untied them. I had gotten up without realizing that somehow the rope that had been keeping me bound was now broken.

"What now?" Sarthak asked us, his leg pressing down onto the woman's throat. He did it so casually. There was something in his eyes.

Pari walked to him and kicked his leg off the woman's throat. The woman coughed. She tried to get up, but Pari kicked her in her stomach.

"Where the hell are we?" Pari continued that sentence with a no-no word.

"What makes you think I'm gonna answer?" the woman laughed in a raspy voice, and twirled her hand.

The room fell away. We were in a big auditorium, with about 15 people spectating us.

Pari stepped back, and the woman got up. She was still heaving for breaths, but smiling, and a moment later, clapping.

She explained while the people, clad in black what-looked-like-HAZMAT suits, watched. "In order to get your magic out, we needed to put you in a stressful situation. None of us expected all of you to go this far, hence me going in with no protection."

"What about our injuries?" Sarthak asked her, touching the area above his eyebrows. The wound was not there. "What the hell?" he whispered. I checked the back of my head. No blood.

"A simulation. I hit you with something similar to what humans call foam."

Before we could ask further questions, she continued. "That nasty, gooey stuff was a stimulant. Don't worry, you won't ever need to touch that again."

I didn't care about that.

"Why did just the four of us and not Hanginton get here?"

She took a moment to answer, because she seemed to be talking to the people in the room looking at us. They were still constantly staring, and it was getting a little weird.

"You had the magic that lets people pass through the chamber. Not Hanginton, not her people."

I was still confused about the point of this whole ordeal. Like, how did they know what triggered our magic? And so many damn illusions. I had no idea what was real and what wasn't. And that landscape. And the volcano. And the corporate building. My mind was spinning.

"What the hell was that thing we were in after being teleported?" Sarthak asked.

"That's the planet we're on. It was the original planet of our kind, until it got destroyed just like your people are destroying yours. Some of us stayed, but most of us went away to other planets, and our magic died out because of some unexplainable reason."

There was a boom in the distance.

Everybody started to run out without a word. The four of us followed them.

"How does our magic even work?" I yelled to ask the woman. "And what's your name?"

"My name is Shay. All of you will have different abilities, I think. There were 8 original warlocks. I don't have the time to tell you about all of them. But your powers will be like theirs. We don't know what your powers are yet, but we'll surely know soon enough."

All of us now were out of the auditorium, and we were on the same landscape we had been on before being put through illusions.

The volcano was experiencing some bad diarrhea. Explosions sprang forth from it, and I could feel the heat even from this far. The volcano's top was barely visible. Even from that far distance, the explosions were very loud.

"Why is everything big here?" I yelled over the explosions.

"We have no clue. Even the tower, made by our ancestors, has no use being this big. We don't even know why it's on Xin."

The tower was in fact not made by accident. The ancestors of these fairies were just big morons.

A ship shot out of the volcano. It was big, and it looked exactly like the ship Hanginton used. Red and blue, just like their uniform.

It landed upon the ground with a loud bang.

Out came people with guns blazing. The fairies tried to fight back, but this was all done in like 5 seconds.

Fire was opened. I saw it all happening in slow motion. Bullets were shot and beams of light were exchanged. But Hanginton's men were triumphant.

Within 3 seconds, everybody except for Shay and the four of us were dead.

Hanginton walked out, huge smirk on her face. She walked over to Shay and kicked her in the stomach.

She mocked Shay. "Long time no see, huh?"

Shay was winded, and before she could get a word out, Hanginton shot her in the forehead. Shay's corpse flopped on the ground.

This was certainly not the ideal situation. My mouth hung open in shock.

Hanginton was pinned onto the ground by Sarthak. The men didn't expect it and didn't have time to react before Sarthak held her in front of him.

He cursed. "Shoot now," he said mockingly.

Magic emanated from the four of us and threw Hanginton the same way we had thrown Shay. She crashed into a rock, and in the corner of my eyes, I saw something approaching.

That thing was another ship, but this one was different than any ship I had ever seen. It was spherical, but had a bump in the front like somebody had taken a bite out of it like it was an apple.

Out of that bump emerged an old-fashioned cannon. It looked like a cannon that would be from earth. But that didn't make sense.

That cannon shot the ground where Hanginton's men were and they disintegrated right before my eyes. I wasn't used to people actually dying in these things. Nobody had actually died up until now, and this was just a bloodbath.

Before that ship could do anything, Hanginton's ship shout out into the sky and disappeared in the blink of an eye.

Our saviors were people I had never seen before, but they were definitely from earth. They ushered for us to get in. None of us spoke a word as we went towards something.

Those poor fairies' corpses were left on the ground as our ship exited the planet, taking us to who knew where.

Hanginton was still somewhere, waiting to strike. She had almost succeeded this time. She had killed innocent people this time. Who knew what she would do the next time.

The people who had rescued her told us that they were Namerians posted on this planet to keep a check on things.

There was a sudden bump and we were in a battleground, on what looked like a big asteroid. Our ship spiraled as we prepared to collide with the ground. I felt the collision in my bones.

"STAY INSIDE!" "WHO DID THIS?" "WHAT THE HELL?" shouts rang left and right as panic struck everybody.

The noises outside the ship were loud. Metal banged, fragments exploded, reinforcements came. This was what Gertrude must have been talking about.

Everything froze. There were loud wooshes as everything crashed into the ground. Our ships exterior exploded, and we were exposed to Hanginton.

I wanted to rip her hair out.

She was by a machine. It looked like a ball machine. I wondered if we were going to have tennis balls thrown at us.

She pressed a button on that machine and the four us flew into the air. The people who had rescued us had disappeared, same way Jammari must have used that chip to get out of H'vannat.

Yellow light came out from our chests, but it grew too much. I saw Hanginton's eyes widening, and her running into some sort of protective dome.

The machine exploded.

In a split second, I saw through the eyes of every Marsian that had my set of powers. I didn't know how I knew. We could manipulate… something. I couldn't tell, and my throat caught up.

But our magic had been unleashed. I felt something that hadn't been there a moment before. A warm glow. The glow of magic.

Epilogue

The Marsian-Whizari war was going nowhere. It was just a huge waste of resources, and a treasure chest for scrappers after the war was done.

The General spent most of the time in his room, going over strategies, resources, people who would be fighting after the machines failed. He was waiting for this to turn into an actual war.

The General felt it in his heart and saw it on his screen. A shockwave that went over the whole asteroid and made its way beyond his ship. His 6000-year-old magic was back. The things he had done to bury the magic of the Marsians had been undone.

But if the magic was back, so were they.

The Ancestors. The people who had been stopped by an ancient order of Warlocks; one the General had been a part of. Only the General had survived the ordeal.

He whimpered in fear of those enormous beings. They were the reason the Marsians had magic, buried deep in their souls.

They would be back for revenge.

They would seek out the General.

Goddamn Hanginton.

THE END

www.ingramcontent.com/pod-product-compliance
Lightning Source LLC
Chambersburg PA
CBHW021205130726
47988CB00002B/513